4/c.

 Aberdeenshire
COUNTY

Aberdeenshire Libraries
www.aberdeenshire.gov.uk/libraries
Renewals Hotline 01224 661511

'You are reluctant to take off your robe,' Raz said softly, 'but once we're married you are going to be naked when you share my bed.'

Layla felt her stomach curl. Everything inside her twisted and heated. She felt dizzy and strange.

Nerves, she thought. 'Does this mean you're agreeing to my suggestion?'

Without warning he lifted a powerful hand and pushed back the swathe of fabric covering her head. His handsome face was taut and unsmiling, as if he were weighing up a decision of enormous importance.

Layla tried not to flinch, even though the gentle brush of those strong fingers against her cheeks made everything inside her clench. She told herself he had every right to look at the woman he might marry.

Her heart started to pound. His forefinger traced the line of her jaw.

His eyes dropped to her mouth.

'You have strength and honesty and I respect those traits.' He rose to his feet, sure and confident and very much the one in control. 'There is no time to lose. We will be married within the hour. Oh, and Princess…' He paused by the entrance to the tent, his eyes a wicked shade of black. 'You have no need of the *Kama Sutra*. When the time comes I will teach you what you need to know.'

LOST TO THE DESERT WARRIOR

BY
SARAH MORGAN

First published in Great Britain 2013
by Mills & Boon, an imprint of Harlequin (UK) Limited.
Harlequin (UK) Limited, Eton House, 18-24 Paradise Road,
Richmond, Surrey TW9 1SR

© Sarah Morgan 2013

ISBN: 978 0 263 23537 1

Harlequin (UK) policy is to use papers that are natural, renewable
and recyclable products and made from wood grown in sustainable
forests. The logging and manufacturing process conform to the
legal environmental regulations of the country of origin.

Printed and bound in Great Britain
by CPI Antony Rowe, Chippenham, Wiltshire

LOST TO THE
DESERT WARRIOR

CHAPTER ONE

*'The Persians teach their sons, between the ages of
five and twenty, only three things: to ride a horse, use
a bow and speak the truth.'*
—from *The Histories by Herodotus*, Greek historian,
about 484-425 BC

'SHH, DON'T MAKE a sound.' Layla slammed her hand over
her sister's mouth. 'I can hear them coming. They mustn't
find us.'

She wished she'd had time to find a better hiding place.
Behind the long velvet curtains in her father's private rooms
hardly seemed like an obvious place for concealment, and
yet she knew in some ways this was the safest place. No
one would think to look for the princesses here. They were
never allowed in his bedroom. Not even today, on the day
of his death.

But Layla had wanted to see for herself that the man who'd
called himself her father lay cold and still in his bed and
wasn't about to leap up and commit some other sin against
her or her sister. She'd stood there, hidden by the curtain, and
heard him seal her fate with his dying breath. His last words
hadn't expressed regret for a life misspent. There had been
no demand to see his daughters, nor even a request to pass
on a loving message to make up for years of cold neglect. No

apology for all the grievous wrongs. Just one last wrong—
one that would seal her fate forever.

*'Hassan must marry Layla. It is the only way the people
will accept him as ruler of Tazkhan.'*

Hearing footsteps, Layla kept her hand pressed over her
younger sister's mouth. Her forehead brushed the curtains and
she could smell the dust. The dark was disorientating and she
held herself rigid, waiting for the curtains to be flung back,
afraid that the slightest movement would give them away.

From behind the protection of rich, heavy velvet she heard
several people enter the room.

'We have searched the palace. They are nowhere to be
found.'

'They cannot just have vanished.' The voice was harsh and
instantly recognisable. It was Hassan, her father's cousin, and
if his last wishes were carried out, soon to be her bridegroom.
Sixty years old and more power-hungry even than her father.

In a moment of horrifying clarity Layla saw her future and
it was blacker than the inside of the curtain. She stared into
darkness, feeling her sister's breath warm her hand, afraid to
breathe herself in case she gave them both away.

'We will find them, Hassan.'

'In a few hours you'll be addressing me as Your Excel-
lency,' Hassan snapped. 'And you'd better find them. Try the
library. The older one is always there. As for the younger
one—she has far too much to say for herself. We're flying her
to America, where she will be out of sight and out of mind.
The people will soon forget her. My marriage to the eldest
will take place before dawn. Fortunately she is the quiet one.
She has nothing to say for herself and is unlikely to object.'

He didn't even know her name, Layla thought numbly, let
alone her view on the world. She was 'the eldest'. 'The quiet
one'. She doubted he knew or cared what she looked like. He
certainly didn't care what she wanted. But then neither had

her father. The only person who cared about her was currently shivering in her grasp.

Her young sister. Her friend. Her *family*.

The news that they were planning to send Yasmin to America intensified the horror of the situation. Of everything that was happening, losing her sister would be the worst.

'Why rush into the marriage?'

Hassan's companion echoed Layla's thoughts.

'Because we both know that as soon as *he* finds out about the old Sheikh's death he will come.'

He will come.

Layla knew immediately who 'he' was. And she also knew Hassan was afraid. So afraid he couldn't bring himself to speak the name of his enemy. The formidable reputation of the desert warrior and rightful ruler of the wild desert country of Tazkhan frightened Hassan so badly it was now forbidden to speak his name within the walled city. The irony was that by banning all mention of the true heir to the sheikdom he had increased his status to that of hero in the minds of the people.

In a small moment of personal rebellion, Layla *thought* the name.

Raz Al Zahki.

A prince who lived like a Bedouin among the people who loved him. A man of the desert with steely determination, strength and patience, who played a waiting game. Right now he was out there somewhere, his exact whereabouts a secret known only to those closest to him. The secrecy surrounding him increased tensions in the Citadel of Tazkhan.

Footsteps echoed on the stone floor of the bedroom.

As the door closed behind them Yasmin pulled away, gasping for air. 'I thought you were going to suffocate me.'

'I thought you were going to scream.'

'I've never screamed in my life. I'm not that pathetic.' But her sister looked shaken and Layla took her hand and held it firmly as she peeped around the heavy velvet curtain.

'They've gone. We're safe.'

'Safe? Layla, that wrinkled, overweight monster is going to marry you before dawn and he's going to send me away to America, miles from home and miles from *you*.'

Layla heard the break in her sister's voice and tightened her grip on her hand. 'No, he won't. I'm not going to allow him to take you away.'

'How can you stop it? I don't care what happens, but I want us to stay together. It's been the two of us for so long I can't imagine any other life. I need you to stop me opening my mouth when I should close it and you need me to stop you living your life in a book.'

Her sister's voice was soaked with despair and Layla felt crushed by the weight of responsibility.

She felt small and powerless as she stood alone against the brutal force of Hassan's limitless ambition.

'I promise we won't be separated.'

'How can you promise that?'

'I don't know yet. But I'm thinking…'

'Well, think fast, because in a few hours I'll be on a plane to America and you'll be in Hassan's bed.'

'Yasmin!' Shocked, Layla gaped at her sister, who shrugged defiantly.

'It's true.'

'What do you know about being in a man's bed?'

'Nowhere near as much as I'd like. I suppose that might be one of the advantages of being banished to America.'

Despite their circumstances, a dimple flickered at the corner of Yasmin's mouth and Layla felt a lump in her throat. No matter how dire the circumstances, her sister always managed to find a reason to smile. She'd brought laughter to places without humour and light into the dark.

'I can't lose you.' She couldn't even bear to think of that option. 'I *won't* lose you.'

Yasmin peered cautiously across the room. 'Is our father really dead?'

'Yes.' Layla tried to find some emotion inside herself but all she felt was numb. 'Are you sad?'

'Why would I be sad? This is only the fifth time I've ever seen him in person and I don't think this one counts so that's only four times. He made our lives hell and he's still making it hell even though he's dead.' Yasmin's unusual blue eyes darkened with fury. 'Do you know what I wish? I wish Raz Al Zahki would ride into the city on that terrifying black stallion of his and finish off Hassan. I'd cheer. In fact I'd be so grateful I'd marry him myself and give him a hundred babies just to make sure his line is safe.'

Layla tried not to look at the figure on the bed. Even dead, she didn't want to see him. 'He wouldn't want to marry you. You are the daughter of the man responsible for the death of his father and his beautiful wife. He hates us, and I cannot blame him for that.' She hated herself too, for sharing the blood of a man with so little humanity. For sharing in his shame.

'He should marry *you*. Then no one would be able to challenge him and Hassan would be finished.'

The idea was so outrageous, so typical of Yasmin, Layla's instinct was to dismiss it instantly and preach caution as she always did. But how was caution going to help them when her marriage was only hours away?

Her mind picked at the idea gingerly. 'Yasmin—'

'It is said he loved his wife so deeply that when she died he made a vow never to love again.' Yasmin spoke in an awed whisper. 'Have you ever heard anything so romantic?'

Layla's courage evaporated along with the idea. *She*

couldn't do it. 'It's not romantic. It's tragic. It was a terrible thing.'

'But to be loved that much by a man as strong and honourable as him—I want that one day.'

Yasmin stared into the distance and Layla gave her a shake.

'Stop dreaming.' The whole thing was alien to her. The only love she knew was her love for her sister. She'd never felt anything remotely romantic when she'd looked at a man. And nothing she'd read on the subject had led her to believe that would change in the future. She was far too practical a person, and it was the practical side that drove her now. 'If they take you to America I'll never see you again. I'm not going to let that happen.'

'How can you stop it? Hassan is at his most dangerous when he's afraid and he's terrified of Raz Al Zahki. He won't even allow his name to be spoken in the city. But everyone *does* speak it, of course. Especially the women. I've been listening.'

'You've been to the *souk* again? Do you have no sense of danger?'

Yasmin ignored her and her voice was an awed whisper. 'They say his heart is frozen into ice and only the right woman can melt it. It's a bit like the legend of the Sword in the Stone you read me when I was little.'

'Oh, Yasmin, grow up! A man's heart cannot be frozen into ice unless he finds himself lost in Antarctica with insufficient equipment. A heart is responsible for pumping blood around the body. It cannot be "frozen" or "broken".' Exasperated, Layla wondered how two sisters could be so different. Their experience was the same, except that Layla had protected Yasmin from the worst of her father's actions. 'This isn't legend, this is *real*. Stop romanticising everything.'

'They think he will come.' This time there was an undertone of excitement in her sister's voice. 'He has been playing a waiting game while our father and Hassan plotted. With our father dead, he has to have a plan for taking up his rightful place as Sheikh. Hassan is terrified. The council is terrified. They have extra guards on the doors at night. They've sent patrols into the desert, although goodness knows why because everyone knows Raz Al Zahki knows the desert better than anyone. No one is sleeping because they're afraid he might enter the Citadel at night and murder them in their beds. Frankly, I wish he'd just get on with it. If I bumped into him in the dark I'd show him the way.'

Layla covered her sister's lips with her fingers. 'You need to be careful what you say.'

'Why? What else can they do to me? They're splitting us up! I'm going to America and you're going to marry Hassan. How much worse can it get?'

'I'm not marrying Hassan.' Layla made her decision. 'I'm not going to let that happen.'

'How can you stop it? Hassan can only be the next ruler if he marries you. That's a pretty powerful motivation.'

'Then he mustn't marry me.'

Yasmin looked at her with pity. 'He is going to make you.'

'If he can't find me, he can't make me.' Not daring to give too much thought to what she was about to do, Layla sprinted to her father's dressing room and removed a couple of robes. She thrust one at her sister. 'Put this on. Cover your hair and as much of your face as you can. Wait here for me behind the curtain until I come and fetch you. I need to get something from the library before we leave.'

'The library? How can you think of books right now?'

'Because a book can be many things—a friend, an escape, a teacher—' Layla broke off and hoped her sister didn't notice her high colour. 'Never mind. The important thing is that we're going away from here. It will be like the game of Hide we played as children.' She caught her sister's horrified glance and wished she hadn't used that reference. Both of them knew what that game had really meant. She changed the subject quickly. 'Those horses you love so much—can you actually ride one if you have to?'

'Of course!'

Her sister's hesitation was so brief Layla told herself she'd imagined it.

'And I've read extensively on the theory of riding and the history of the Arabian horse, so between us I'm sure we'll be fine.' She hoped she sounded more convincing than she felt. 'We'll take the back route to the stables and ride into the desert from there.'

'The desert? Why are we riding into the desert?'

Layla felt her mouth move even though her brain was telling her this was a terrible idea. 'We're going to find Raz Al Zahki.'

The wind blew across the desert, bringing with it whispers of the Sheikh's death.

Raz Al Zahki stood at the edge of the camp and stared into the darkness of the night. 'Is it truth or rumour?'

'Truth.' Salem stood next to him, shoulder to shoulder. 'It's been confirmed by more than one source.'

'Then it is time.' Raz had learned long before to keep his feelings buried, and he kept them buried now, but he felt the familiar ache of tension across his shoulders. 'We leave for the city tonight.'

Abdul, his advisor and long-time friend stepped forward. 'There is something else, Your Highness. As you predicted, Hassan plans to marry the eldest princess in a matter of hours. Preparations for the wedding are already underway.'

'Before her father's body is even cold?' Raz gave a cynical laugh. 'Her grief clearly overwhelms her.'

'Hassan must be at least forty years older than her,' Salem murmured. 'One wonders what she gains from the match.'

'There is no mystery there. She continues to live in a palace and enjoy benefits that should never have been hers to begin with.' Raz stared at the horizon. 'She is the daughter of the most ruthless man who ever ruled Tazkhan. Don't waste your sympathy.'

'If Hassan marries the girl it will be harder for you to challenge the succession legally.'

'Which is why I intend to make sure the wedding does not take place.'

Abdul shot him a startled look. 'So you intend to go ahead with your plan? Even though what you're suggesting is—'

'The only option available.' Raz cut him off, hearing the hardness in his own tone. It was the same hardness that ran right through him. Once, he'd been capable of warmth, but that part of him had died along with the woman he'd loved. 'We have considered every other option, and—' He broke off as he heard a commotion in the darkness and then lifted a hand as his bodyguards emerged silently to flank him.

They were men who had followed him for fifteen years, since the brutal slaying of his father. Men who would die for him.

Abdul thrust himself in front of Raz and that gesture touched him more than any other, because his trusted advisor was neither physically fit nor skilled with weapons.

Gently, but firmly, he moved him to one side, but Abdul protested.

'Go. *Go*! It could be the attempt on your life we have been expecting.'

Aware that Salem had his hand on his weapon, Raz fixed his gaze on the slim figure of a boy whose arms were gripped by two of his men. 'If my death were the objective then surely they would give the responsibility to someone I could not so easily crush.'

'We found him wandering in the desert along the border with Zubran. He appears to be alone. He says he has a message for Raz Al Zahki.'

Knowing that his men were protecting his identity, Raz signalled for them to bring their captive forward.

His hands were tied and as they released him the boy stumbled and fell to his knees. Raz stared down at him, noticing absently that his robes swamped his thin body.

It was Salem who spoke. Salem, his brother, who rarely left his side. 'What message do you have for Raz Al Zahki, boy?'

'I have to speak to him in person.' The words were mumbled and barely audible. 'And I have to be alone when I do it. What I have to say is just for him and no other.'

The guard closest to him gave a grunt of disgust. 'Someone like you wouldn't get close enough to Raz Al Zahki to wave from a distance, let alone be alone with him, and you should be grateful for that. He'd eat you alive.'

'I don't care what he does to me as long as he hears what I have to say. Take me to him. *Please.*'

The boy kept his head bowed and something in the set of those narrow shoulders drew Raz's attention.

Ignoring Salem's attempts to hold him back, he stepped forward. 'So you're not afraid?'

There was a brief pause. The wind blew across the desert, whipping up sand and catching the edges of the boy's robe. He clutched it desperately.

'Yes, I am afraid. But not of Raz Al Zahki.'

'Then you need to be educated.' The guard dragged his captive to his feet and the boy gasped in pain. 'We'll keep him here tonight and question him again in the morning.'

'No!' The boy struggled frantically in the man's grip. 'By

morning it will be too late. I have to speak to him now. Please. The future of Tazkhan depends on it.'

Raz stared at the boy, half shrouded by robes that were too big for him. 'Take him to my tent.'

Salem, Abdul and the guards looked at him in disbelief.

'Do it,' Raz said softly, but still the guards hesitated.

'We'll strip-search him first—'

'Take him to my tent and then leave us.'

Abdul touched his arm, his voice low. 'I have never before questioned your decisions, Your Highness, but this time I beg you, at least keep the guards with you.'

'You think I can't defend myself from someone half my height and weight?'

'I think Hassan will try anything at this late stage in the game. He is frightened and desperate and a desperate man should never be underestimated. I think it could be a trap.'

'I agree.' Salem's voice was hard. 'I'll come with you.'

Raz put his hand on his brother's shoulder. 'Your love and loyalty means more to me than you can possibly know, but you must trust me.'

'If anything happened to you—'

Raz felt the weight of it settle onto his shoulders. He, better than anyone, knew that there were some promises that shouldn't be made. 'Make sure I'm not disturbed.' He dismissed his bodyguards with a single movement of his hand and strode into his tent.

He closed the flap, muffling the sound of the wind and protecting them from prying eyes.

The boy was on his knees in the furthest corner of the tent, his hands still tied.

Raz studied him for a moment and then strolled over to him and cut the rope with a swift movement of his knife. 'Stand up.'

The boy hesitated and then stood in a graceful movement, only to fall again a moment later.

'I don't think I can stand—' The words were uttered through clenched teeth. 'My legs are stiff from riding and I injured my ankle when I fell.'

Raz looked down at the slender body bowed at his feet. 'Tell me why you're here.'

'I'll talk to Raz Al Zahki himself, and no one else.'

'Then speak,' Raz commanded softly, and the boy lifted his head in shock.

Under the concealing robes, dark eyes widened. 'You're him?'

'I'm the one asking the questions.' Raz sheathed his knife. 'And the first thing I want to know is what a woman is doing creeping around my camp in the middle of the night. What are you doing walking into the lion's den unprotected, Princess?'

Layla was in agony. Physical agony from her fall from the horse, and emotional agony from the knowledge that her sister was missing and alone in the vast emptiness of the baking desert and it was all her fault.

She was the one who had suggested this stupid, crazy plan. She, who never did anything stupid or crazy. She, who studied all available evidence before she made a decision, had acted on impulse. Which just proved that a cautious nature wasn't to be mocked.

It would have been better had Hassan sent Yasmin to America. At least then Layla would have known she was alive.

As it was, Yasmin was lost, and she was now a captive in the desert camp of Raz Al Zahki, a man who had more reason to hate her than any other.

A man who knew who she was.

Staring into those cold black eyes, she suddenly knew the meaning of the phrase 'between a rock and a hard place.' If her cousin was the hard place then this man was the rock. He stood legs spread, handsome face unsmiling as he stared at her. His body had the muscular structure of a warrior's, his shoulders broad and hard. She knew he had suffered terribly and yet there was no sign of suffering in face. This man wasn't broken, he was whole and strong—at least on the outside. There was nothing soft about him. Nothing vulnerable. Even before he'd revealed his identity she'd sensed his place at the head of the pack. He had the confidence and authority of a man born to lead others, and even though Layla had expected nothing less still he intimidated her.

'You knew who I was the whole time?'

'Within five seconds. You have a memorable face, Princess. And very distinctive eyes.'

It was the first personal comment anyone had ever made to her and it took her by surprise.

She'd studied him on paper and committed all the facts to memory, from his year and place of birth to his impressive military career and his degree in engineering. She knew he was a skilled rider and an authority on the Arabian horse. She knew all that, but was only just realising that facts could only tell you so much about a man.

They couldn't tell you that his eyes were darker than the desert at night or that the power he commanded on paper was surpassed a thousand times by the power he commanded in person. They couldn't tell you that those eyes were capable of seeing right through a person to the very centre of their being. They couldn't tell you that meeting those eyes would make your heart thunder like the hooves of a hundred wild horses pounding across the desert plain.

She was fast realising that a list of dates and qualifications didn't convey strength or charisma.

Unsettled that the facts had given her such an incomplete picture, Layla remembered what her sister had said about the rumours. That Raz Al Zahki was a man who knew women. Before he'd fallen in love he'd been wild, and afterwards he'd locked it all away. Every emotion. Every feeling.

'How do you know me?'

'I make a point of knowing my enemy.'

'I am not your enemy.' And yet she could hardly blame him for thinking that, could she? His family had suffered terribly at the hands of hers. They stood on opposite sides of an enormous rift that had divided their families for generations.

'Which brings me to my second question—where is Hassan? Or is he so lacking in courage he sends a woman with his messages?'

Layla shivered, but whether it was his tone or his words that affected her she didn't know.

'I'm not here because of Hassan. I was with my sister, Yasmin, but I fell from the horse.' She saw his beautiful mouth tighten. 'I'm sorry—I—you have to help me find her. *Please.* She's alone in the desert and she won't have a clue how to survive.' The thought filled her with despair but still he showed no emotion. No sympathy. Nothing.

'So where is Hassan?'

'He could be back at the palace, or he could be out there looking for us. I don't know.'

'You don't know? And yet this is the man you're supposed to be marrying in a matter of hours.'

And if Hassan found Yasmin first—

His words slowly seeped into her numb brain. 'You know about the wedding?'

'I know everything.'

'If you think I want to marry Hassan then clearly you *don't* know everything.' The tent was dimly lit, but there was enough light for her to see the flash of surprise in his eyes.

'How did you leave, if not with his consent?'

'We escaped. My sister loves horses. She took the fastest horse in the stables. Unfortunately she omitted to tell me she couldn't control him.' Layla rubbed her palm across her bruised back. 'He proved too much for both of us.'

'*Both* of you?' A dark eyebrow lifted. 'You rode one horse?'

'Yes. We're not that heavy and we didn't want to be separated.' Layla didn't tell him that she'd never ridden before. This man was renowned for his horsemanship. She had a feeling he wouldn't be impressed by the fact she knew everything about the breeding history of the Arabian horse, but nothing about the reality of riding one. 'Something scared him and he reared up. I fell and he bolted with Yasmin on his back. She won't be strong enough to stop him. She's probably fallen, too.' Panicking, she tried to stand up again, but her body protested so violently she sank back onto her knees just as two large dogs bounded into the tent.

Terror sucked the strength from her limbs. She was at eye level with the two beasts as they came to a standstill, teeth bared.

Raz said something to them and they whimpered and sank down to their bellies, huge eyes fixed on him in adoration.

'Saluki?' The fear was so sharp Layla could hardly breathe. 'You own Saluki?'

'You recognise the breed?'

'Of course.' Her mouth felt as if she'd swallowed all the sand in the desert. If dogs could smell fear, she was doomed. 'The Saluki is one of the oldest breeds in existence. They have been found in the Pyramids of Egypt, mummified alongside the bodies of pharaohs.' She didn't reveal that her familiarity with the breed came from a darker, more personal experience. An experience she'd tried to block from her mind.

'You said you were escaping. What was your destination?'

'You. You were my destination.' Reminding herself that the dogs were unlikely to attack without provocation or command, Layla kept utterly still, watching the animals. 'We were trying to find you.'

'On the night your father died? From the lack of tears it would seem you have inherited his lack of sentimentality.'

Was that what he thought?

Shocked, Layla almost corrected him, but she knew this wasn't the right time. Misunderstandings could be corrected later. Or maybe they didn't even matter. 'It was my father's dying wish that I marry Hassan.'

The darkening of his eyes was barely perceptible. 'So why come looking for me?'

She'd practised a hundred alternative ways to say what she wanted to say but every word vanished under that icy scrutiny. 'You are the rightful ruler, but if he marries me that weakens your claim and strengthens his.'

There was a sudden stillness about him that suggested she had his full attention. 'That still doesn't tell me why you're here.'

Only now did Layla realise just how much she'd been hoping he'd be the one to say it. He was praised for his intelligence, wasn't he? Couldn't he see for himself why she was here? Couldn't he see the one solution that would solve this once and for all?

But perhaps he could see and chose not to look.

'I don't blame you for hating us.' The words tumbling out of her mouth weren't the ones she'd rehearsed but when she looked at him all she could think of was the loss he'd suffered. 'If I could change who I am then I would, but I'm asking you to put that aside and do what needs to be done.'

'And what,' he prompted softly, 'do you believe needs to be done, Princess?'

No man had ever asked her opinion. Not once since the day she took her first step to the day she and her sister had slid out of the window of their father's bedroom. Not once had anyone treated her as anything but a weapon in the considerable armory of the house of Al Habib.

But this man had asked her.

This man was listening to her.

He was regal, she thought, proud and sure of himself. In that moment she caught a glimpse of why so many trusted him and protected him. He was as different from Hassan as the ocean from the desert.

'You *know* what needs to be done. You have to take your rightful place. You have to end this before Hassan finishes what my father started. Before he ruins our country in the selfish pursuit of power...' She paused, wondering whether to mention Yasmin again but deciding this man would be motivated more by his duty to his people than sympathy for her sister. 'And to do that you have to marry me. Now. Quickly. Before Hassan finds me and takes me back.'

CHAPTER TWO

HE'D BEEN PLANNING to do whatever was necessary to prevent her wedding to Hassan taking place. Yet he had not considered the option of marrying her himself, nor had any of those surrounding him dared to suggest it despite the fact it was the obvious solution.

The tactician in him could see the benefit. The man in him recoiled.

He'd thought there was no price he wouldn't pay to fulfil his duty.

He'd been wrong.

Tension rippled down his spine. He felt as if he were being strangled.

'No.' He'd trained himself to shut down emotion but that skill suddenly failed him and his refusal came from somewhere deep inside him. Some dark part of himself he no longer accessed. 'I had a wife. I don't need or want another.' His voice sounded strange. Thickened by a hundred layers of personal agony. One of the dogs growled, a threatening sound that came from low in the animal's throat. He saw her gaze flicker to the dog and sensed her fear although he didn't understand it.

'I know about your wife.' Her brief hesitation suggested she was about to say something else on that topic, but then she gave a little shake of her head. 'Obviously I'm not sug-

gesting myself as a replacement. This would be purely a political arrangement, advantageous to both sides.'

Raz tried to detach his mind from the pain he carried
around inside himself. 'Political?'

'Hassan's position is precarious. Marriage to me is his way
of securing his place as my father's successor. He has no support in Tazkhan and has never taken the trouble to earn it. For
him, ruling is about what he can gain rather than what he can
give and that approach makes him neither popular nor secure.'

Raz hid his surprise. He'd listened to men talk for hours
on the problems facing Tazkhan and yet this girl had sum-
marised the situation in four blunt sentences, devoid of emotion, exaggeration or drama.

'Perhaps he didn't expect your father to die so soon.'

Again there was hesitation, and it was obvious she was
being selective about what she told him. 'Hassan knows that
the only way he will be accepted is to marry me, and he is
willing to do anything to make that happen. Do not underestimate him.'

Her words were like the scrape of a knife over an open
wound because he'd done exactly that. In his righteous arro-
gance he'd thought himself untouchable and as a result he'd
lost someone he'd loved deeply.

'You seem very familiar with the workings of his mind.'

'I've studied him. I think there is a strong chance he is clin-
ically disturbed. He demonstrates some of the elements of a
sociopath, shows no remorse or guilt for any of his actions.'

Her words were serious, those beautiful, almond-shaped
eyes steady on his.

'He has no care for the feelings or opinions of others and
an overinflated idea of his own importance. He is a dangerous man. But you already know that.'

'Yes.' He did know. What surprised him was that *she* knew.

Raz realised he'd made assumptions about her based purely

on her bloodline. He also knew she was right that the marriage had to be prevented. He didn't reveal that he'd had his own plans for making sure it didn't happen.

There was no doubt her plan was better. Permanent.

And safer for all concerned.

Except for him.

For him, it meant breaking a vow.

His tension levels soaring into the stratosphere, Raz paced the length of the tent.

Whichever way he looked at it, it felt like a betrayal. It pulled him down and tore at him. 'I cannot do it.'

'Because I am the daughter of your enemy?' She spoke in the same calm voice. 'Aristotle said "a common danger unites the bitterest of enemies". We have a common danger. I am proposing we unite. It is the right thing to do and you know it.'

Raz turned with a snarl that drew the dogs to their feet. 'Never assume to guess what I am thinking, Princess.'

Her head was slightly bowed but he could see her eyes were fixed in terror on the two animals now crouched low on the floor of the tent.

'I beg your pardon.' She held herself absolutely still, her voice barely more than a whisper. 'It seems a logical solution to me. I assumed it would seem so to you.'

It did. The fact that his emotions defied logic frustrated him. 'Do you apply logic to everything?'

'I didn't apply logic when I chose to steal a horse and point him towards the desert, so the answer has to be no, not to everything. But to most things. I find generally the outcome is better if the action is given the appropriate consideration.'

He'd never met anyone as serious as her.

He wanted to ask if she'd ever laughed, danced or had fun, and then wondered why he was even interested.

'You are suggesting something I cannot contemplate.'

'And yet you know it is the right thing for Tazkhan. So

your reluctance must be because you once had a wife you loved so very much.'

Raz felt the blood drain from his face. The tips of his fingers were suddenly cold. Anger sharpened his brain and tongue. 'Logic, if not an instinct for self-preservation, should be warning you that you are now treading on ground that is likely to give way beneath your feet.'

'I did not bring up that topic to cause you pain, but to try and understand why you would say no to something that is so obviously right.' Her fingers shook as she smoothed the robe she was wearing. 'You loved her and exchanged promises, and now you never want to marry again. I understand that.'

'You understand nothing.' He heard the growl in his own voice. 'You have condensed a thousand indescribable emotions into one short sentence.' The force of his anger shook him, and it clearly shook her too because her eyes flickered to the entrance of the tent, gauging the distance. Raz felt a rush of shame because whatever his sins, and God knew there had been many, frightening women wasn't one of them.

She spoke before he did. 'I'm sorry.' Her tone was a soothing balm against the raw edges of his pain. 'And you're right, of course. I don't understand what you're feeling because I've never loved anyone that way. But I understand that what you lost is somehow linked with your decision never to marry again. And I just want to make clear that what I'm suggesting has nothing to do with what you had before. Ours would be a marriage of political necessity, not of love. Not a betrayal of her memory, but a business arrangement. If you marry me, you take your rightful place as ruler of Tazkhan. You would be unchallenged.'

Not a betrayal of her memory.

So maybe she did understand him better than he'd first thought.

'You think I'm afraid of a challenge?'

'No. But I know you love your people and want to give Tazkhan a peaceful and prosperous future.' Suddenly she sounded very tired, very alone and very young.

Raz frowned as he tried to remember her age. Twenty-three? Younger?

'And what do you gain from this arrangement, Princess? How do you benefit from entering into a marriage where feelings play no part?' In the flickering candlelight he could see a hint of smooth cheek beneath the voluminous robes, but very little else except those eyes. And her eyes were mesmerising—as dark as sloes and framed by long, thick lashes that shadowed that smooth skin like the setting sun. Suddenly he wanted to see more of her. He wanted to reach out and rip off the robes that concealed her and see what lay beneath the folds of fabric. He'd heard whispers about the beauty of the elder princess and ignored them all because her physical attributes had been of no interest to him.

Disturbed by the sudden flare of his own curiosity, he stepped back. 'How do you benefit from this "business arrangement"?'

'If I am married to you, then I cannot be married to Hassan.'

'So I am the lesser of two evils?' Could that truly be the reason? Raz struggled to decipher her intentions. She seemed innocent and yet she came from evil. She appeared to speak the truth but those who surrounded her spoke only lies. Feeling the weight of responsibility, he suppressed his instinct to trust her. 'You are expecting me to believe that you crept out of the Citadel tonight, stole a horse and rode aimlessly into the desert in the hope of tripping over me so that you could propose marriage?'

'I had more to lose by staying than leaving. And it is well known that there are plenty of people who know your whereabouts, Your Highness. I trusted that someone would bring me to you.'

She'd called him 'Your Highness'. It was an acknowledgement he wouldn't have expected from her, given that they were on opposite sides.

Raz narrowed his eyes. 'Your loyalties are easily shifted.'

'My loyalties are to Tazkhan, but I understand that you are afraid to trust me. I do have other reasons—more personal ones.'

'What other reasons?'

'If he finds her, Hassan intends to send my sister to America.' Desperation shook that steady voice. 'He wants her out of the way.'

'Why would he want her out of the way?'

'Because we are stronger together than we are apart and he wants to weaken us. Because my sister has an uncomfortable habit of speaking her mind and she becomes harder to control with each passing day. She is dreamy, passionate, and challenges everything. And Hassan hates to be challenged.'

'And you don't challenge him?'

'I see no point in poking an angry dragon with a stick.'

'And where is your sister now?'

'I don't know.' There was fear and anxiety under the veneer of calm. 'The horse galloped off. I'm scared she might have fallen and been injured. I'm scared Hassan's men will find her before you do.'

Raz lifted an eyebrow. 'That is almost inevitable since I'm not looking for her.'

'But *will* you look for her? Once I'm your bride, will you also offer your protection to my sister?'

So that was why she was here, he thought.

She'd risked everything for love. Not romantic love, perhaps, but love all the same.

'So to keep your sister with you, and protect Tazkhan, you

would marry a stranger. That is the least romantic proposition I have ever heard.'

'Possibly. But we've already established this is not about romance. You wouldn't want that and neither would I.'

'Why wouldn't you?'

'I am not a romantic person, Your Highness.'

That matter-of-fact statement might have been unremarkable had it come from someone several decades older than she was. Her eyes were dark, luminous pools of pain and he wondered how those eyes would look if she smiled.

'You don't believe there can be love between a man and a woman?'

'Yes, I do believe there can be. Just not for me. I'm not like that. I don't have those feelings. I'm a very practical person,' she said with disarming honesty. 'As you don't want love either, I assume that won't be an obstacle for you.' She brushed it aside as easily as the desert winds shifted sand.

She had no idea, he thought. No idea that love was the most powerful force known to man. No idea how much havoc could be wrought by that emotion.

But *he* knew.

He'd been caught in the wake of devastation and still ached from his injuries.

'You say that this is a political arrangement to secure the future of Tazkhan, but for a marriage to be legal and binding in our country it requires more than simply the exchange of vows and rings.'

Her spine was rigid and her eyes were fixed on the ground in front of him. 'I am aware of that. It's important that Hassan isn't able to challenge our union so I've already familiarised myself with Tazkhan marriage laws.'

Raz found himself intrigued and exasperated in equal measures. 'So you understand what marriage entails?'

'You're referring to the physical side and, yes, I understand that. I know it has to be a full and proper marriage. I accept that. It won't be a problem.' She'd dipped her head so that the folds of her robe almost obscured her features. 'From what I've read, it shouldn't be a problem for you, either. A man doesn't need love in order to be able to perform the sexual act.'

'Perform?' Raz was torn between amusement and disbelief as he stared down at her. Under the protective folds of the robe she was shy, fragile and clueless. 'What exactly have you been reading? Whatever it is, it sounds an unusual choice for a girl like you.'

'I'm not a girl. I'm a woman.'

Not yet. The thought flew into his head and he stared at her for a long moment.

'You are contemplating a lifetime with a man who cannot love you.'

'But you will respect me.' Lifting her head, she looked him directly in the eyes. 'You will respect me for making the decision to do the right thing for Tazkhan. And that is all I need.'

Raz stared at her for a long moment.

Respect.

Was that really all she needed?

It sounded like very little, and yet right now he wasn't sure he could deliver even that.

Feeling the weight of responsibility pressing down on him like a thousand tons of sand, he turned and strode to the doorway of the tent. 'I need air.'

I need air.

Layla sagged. She needed air, too. She couldn't breathe. She was suffocating under the heavy fabric of the robes and the stifling heat in the tent and she was terrified she'd blown everything by mentioning his wife. And as for the rest of it— she'd never thought talking about sex could feel so uncomfortable. It was a natural act, performed by animals—of which man was one—since the dawn of time. Why a discussion on the topic should leave her hot and shaky she had no idea.

It was *him*.

There was something about him—a raw physicality that made her understand for the first time why women talked about him in dreamy tones.

Confused, exhausted and desperately worried about Yasmin, all Layla wanted was to strip off the robes she'd taken from her father's rooms and lie down.

She looked longingly at the low bed covered in richly coloured silks that dominated the far side of the tent.

His bed?

Just for a moment she had an image of him lying there, strong limbs entwined with the beauty who had been his wife, sharing their love. The image shocked her. Apart from images of the sculptures of Michelangelo she'd never seen a man naked, so she had no reason to be imagining one now.

Her body ached from head to foot and she wanted to stretch her limbs and examine her bruises, but she was too afraid to move with the dogs guarding her.

She watched them as she carefully tried to ease herself into a different position.

The bag she'd tied under the robes pressed uncomfortably against her hip and she pulled out the two books she'd taken from the library. One was her favourite—a book she'd read so many times she almost knew it by heart. The other—

'What is that?' His voice came from the doorway of the tent and Layla jumped and dropped both books onto the thick rug that carpeted the floor of the tent.

'Books. Just books. I brought them from home.'

Before she could snatch them back he stooped and picked one up. And of course it was *that* one.

There was a tense silence while he scanned the title of

the volume. Dark eyebrows rose in incredulity. 'The *Kama Sutra*?'

'If I'm proposing marriage then it's important I have some knowledge of what is required. There is no skill that cannot be mastered with sufficient studying. I'm ignorant, and in my experience ignorance is never bliss.'

She could hear the blood throbbing in her ears. She felt her mouth dry as if she had swallowed all the sand in the desert and her heart pounded like the hooves of the Arabian stallion who had thrown her onto the sand with such disdain.

His prolonged silence was more humiliating than a refusal and she was grateful for the semi-darkness of the tent that gave her at least some protection from his scrutiny.

Her expectations of this encounter had been modest. She hadn't exactly expected him to embrace the idea of marriage with enthusiasm, but she'd thought he'd say *something*. She certainly hadn't expected him to walk out of the tent.

But perhaps the thought of marrying her sickened him. Perhaps people were wrong and Raz Al Zahki *wouldn't* do anything that needed to be done for his country. Perhaps even he wouldn't stoop so low as to marry the daughter of the man who had destroyed his family.

Perhaps he didn't want a woman whose knowledge of the world had been gained from the contents of her father's library.

'You're not going to need this.' He handed the book back to her and her face burned like the desert in the midday heat

Tears formed a hot burning ball in the back of her throat and she almost choked on it.

He was refusing to marry her.

'I understand. In that case I need to try and find my sister myself, before Hassan does. He is at his most dangerous when he is angry and he will be very angry.' She struggled to her feet, but her legs cramped from kneeling for so long in one position and she lost her balance.

He caught her and scooped her into his arms.

Afraid of being dropped to the ground for the second time in one day, Layla gripped his shoulders and her fingers dug into an unyielding layer of solid muscle.

In her day-to-day life at the palace she didn't encounter men like him. Her father had surrounded himself with men like Hassan: men whose flesh was softened from inactivity, sycophants whose purpose in life was to indulge to the fullest.

She doubted Raz Al Zahki had ever overindulged in his life. He was lean, athletic, super-fit—and dangerous in every way.

As she turned her head, her eyes met the fierce black of his. Curiosity turned to fascination. Her eyes dropped to his mouth, now terrifyingly close to hers. Hassan's mouth was full and fleshy, but this man's lips were firm and perfectly shaped. His face was beauty blended with hardness. Hardness in the savage slash of his cheekbones and the lean line of his darkened jaw. Hardness in the grim set of his mouth and the glint in his eyes. And that hardness gave him an edge of danger. Even she, with no expertise or interest in men, could see why women might describe him as spectacularly handsome.

Something tightened deep in her stomach. Heat washed across her skin and poured through her veins.

They stared at each other and then his mouth compressed. He strode across the tent and lowered her onto the silken cover draped over the large bed, standing over her, powerful and imposing in every way.

'Where does it hurt? Explain your injuries.'

That curt command jolted her out of her dreamy state of contemplation.

Layla told herself there was no reason to feel intimidated. He couldn't help his height. He couldn't help his powerful build. And she could hardly blame him for not smiling in the circumstances.

He'd asked about her injuries.

All the talk of romance and emotions had stressed her beyond belief, so the practical nature of his question soothed her. She preferred the definable to the indefinable and her injuries were definitely definable.

'I ache all over, but particularly my legs, my back and my arms. I suspect it's a mixture of stiffness from unaccustomed muscle use and bruising from the fall. Based on the symptoms, I don't believe anything is broken.'

His eyes gleamed with irony. 'Presumably you have studied medical texts along with Aristotle and the *Kama Sutra*? Your reading matter is diverse, Princess.'

She didn't tell him she hadn't even started the *Kama Sutra*. 'I read a lot.'

'You read. Your sister talks.' He studied her for several long and deeply unsettling minutes. 'Take the robe off.'

'What?' Feeling like a tiny mouse in the sights of a predatory eagle, Layla stared at him. 'Why?'

'Because I want to assess the state of your injuries for myself.'

'I don't have any injuries,' she said quickly. 'Truly, it's just muscular. Superficial. Nothing for you to worry about but I appreciate your concern.' She'd been desperate to be out of the robes, but now she was equally desperate to keep them on. The thought of removing them in front of this man unsettled her.

With a sigh he sat down on the bed, his thigh brushing briefly against hers. 'You say you want marriage and yet you're afraid even to remove your robe in my presence? Are you proposing that once we're married we go to bed fully clothed?'

'No, of course not. That's different.'

'*How* is it different?'

He was testing her. He thought she couldn't do it.

Desperation blew away modesty. If he refused to marry her she would never see Yasmin again.

'I will be fine. I will take the responsibilities that come with the role very seriously.'

'Responsibilities?'

'Physical intimacy is one of the responsibilities of a wife. I understand that. I understand exactly what is involved.'

'Are you sure?' Those dark eyes swept her face with disturbing intensity. 'How much of the *Kama Sutra* have you read, Princess?'

If she said she'd read the whole thing cover to cover would he marry her?

Layla opened her mouth and then closed it again, because she knew her skills at lying were on a par with her horse-riding abilities. 'Not much.' She hoped honesty wasn't going to kill her future. 'In fact just the title so far. But I'm a fast reader,' she added quickly, afraid that her lack of knowledge might put him off. 'And *you* have experience.'

For some reason just saying that made her body warm.

Because looking at his face made her feel hot and uncomfortable she stared instead at his hands, but for some reason that didn't make her feel any better. She felt as if she'd had a shot of adrenaline straight into the heart.

'You are reluctant to take off your robe,' he said softly, 'but once we're married you are going to be naked when you share my bed.'

Layla felt her stomach curl. Everything inside her twisted and heated. She felt dizzy and strange.

Nerves, she thought. 'Does this mean you're agreeing to my suggestion?'

Without warning he lifted a powerful hand and pushed back the swath of fabric covering her head. His handsome face was taut and unsmiling, as if he were weighing up a decision of enormous importance.

Layla tried not to flinch even though the gentle brush of those strong fingers against her cheeks made everything inside her clench. She told herself he had every right to look at the woman he might marry.

Was he looking to see if she were as beautiful as his wife? Or was he deciding if he could look upon her every day and not see the face of her father and Hassan and think of the destruction they'd caused in his life.

He continued to look, his gaze disturbingly intense as his fingers trailed slowly over her cheek.

She knew her face was flushed. She could feel the heat and knew he would be able to feel it, too, with those fingers that seemed in no hurry to cease their exploration of her skin.

Her heart started to pound.

The seconds passed and a minute became two minutes and longer.

His forefinger traced the line of her jaw.

His eyes dropped to her mouth.

Layla was rigid with discomfort. She had no idea of the correct etiquette in this situation. Was she supposed to do something? Say something? Was it some sort of test?

She remembered Yasmin telling her that his wife had been stunningly beautiful.

Was this all about comparison?

When he spoke, there was something in his tone she couldn't identify. 'You are brave.'

Torn between relief that there was at least one thing about her he liked and disappointment that such close examination hadn't uncovered anything else to commend her, Layla felt obliged to tell the truth. 'I'm not very brave. I ran away from the palace.'

'And you ran to me and offered me everything, even though deep down the thought of it frightens you.'

'I'm not frightened.'

'So far I believe you have been honest with me. I advise you not to change that.'

She hesitated. 'I don't think you'll hurt me.'

His eyes darkened. 'I will inevitably hurt you—as you would know if you'd read the book.'

Was he talking physically? Out of her depth in a conversation that felt like a swim in boiling oil, Layla had never felt more mortified in her life. 'If there is pain then I'll bear it.'

'You seem determined to pursue this course, but what you are proposing will tie us together for a lifetime, so I urge you to think carefully and be sure this is what you want.'

'That's why I came to you and suggested it.' Surely the facts spoke for themselves? Why did he keep asking her? 'The alternative is being tied to Hassan for a lifetime and you must see that lacks appeal for so many reasons.'

There was a glimmer of something in his eyes. It might have been admiration or it might have been pity or even humour.

'You have strength and honesty and I respect those traits. If respect is truly all you need from a relationship then I can promise you that. It will be done.' He rose to his feet, sure and confident and very much the one in control. 'I will send Salem to find your sister and instruct him to bring her here. I agree that there is no time to lose, so you and I will be married within the hour. I will send someone to help you prepare. Oh, and princess…' He paused by the entrance to the tent, his eyes a wicked shade of black. 'You have no need of that book. When the time comes I will teach you what you need to know.'

CHAPTER THREE

'I AM TO search for a princess who talks too much? What sort of a description is that? Every woman I know talks too much.' Salem sat relaxed on his horse, a look of incredulity on his handsome face as he looked at his brother. 'If the stallion she stole is the one we think it is, he was bred for speed and endurance. He could have carried her for miles. She could be anywhere. Or lying dead somewhere in the desert.'

'The fact that she talks too much should make her all the easier to find and we both know that with your abilities you can track anyone.' Raz rode alongside him, controlling a horse who snorted and pawed at the sand, yearning for speed. 'Be careful. Hassan will be looking for her and the horse. And also for you.'

'And for *you*. You should not be asking me to leave you at this time.'

'I'm not asking you. I'm giving you an order.'

'Is it true that you are going to marry the Princess tonight?'

Salem's voice was soft and Raz kept his hand steady as he soothed the horse.

'It is the right thing to do. The only thing.'

'It may be the right thing for Tazkhan, but is it right for *you*?'

Raz ignored the question. 'You will do everything in your power to find the younger sister.'

'You vowed never to marry again.'

No one but his brother would have dared make such a personal remark and the words were like the sharp flick of a whip.

'There is more than one type of marriage. This will be a marriage of the head, not of the heart.'

'And the Princess?' There was a creak of leather as Salem shifted his position in the saddle. 'She's young. Is that the life she wants?'

'She claims that it is.'

'Does she know about—?'

'No.' Raz interrupted him before he could finish the sentence. 'But she understands exactly what I am able to offer her.'

'And you trust her? You can live with her, knowing who she is?'

'I will learn to live with her.' He blocked thoughts of her heritage and instead thought of her sitting huddled on his bed, gripping the oversized robe in clenched hands. He thought of the book she'd chosen to bring from the library to equip her for her new role. *Thought of the courage it must have taken to come to him.* 'She has very little life experience.'

'Whereas you have decades too much. You're not an easy man to know, Raz—are you being fair to her?'

'I will endeavour to be as fair as possible.' Frowning, Raz released his hold on the reins and urged the stallion forward. 'You're wasting time. The key to my bride's happiness will be finding her sister safe and well. Make that happen.'

Salem rode away from him. 'Just watch your back, brother.'

'His Highness instructed us to bring you clothes.' The girl dropped a dress on the bed. Resentment and animosity throbbed from her and it was obvious she wished she had not been the one chosen for the task.

'Thank you.' Having washed away the dust from her fall in the water that had been hastily provided, Layla stared at the exquisite fall of silk, caught at the waist with a silver belt. 'I didn't expect a dress.' Especially not a dress like this one. *A romantic dress.* Where had he found it?

She remembered his comment about romance and felt a flash of panic that Raz Al Zahki would think she was secretly nurturing dreams about their relationship, and then remembered that he was the last person to encourage such a delusion.

He didn't want this any more than she did.

'You cannot marry His Highness in dusty robes that swamp you. You have to look your best on your wedding day.' There was censorship in her tone and something else. *Jealousy?*

Feeling desperately alone, Layla missed her sister more than ever. She suppressed the urge to point out there was no reason for anyone to feel jealous. That this marriage was driven by loyalty to his country and no other emotion.

Surely it was obvious?

'The Sheikh and I met for the first time a few hours ago.'

'But you have been chosen as the one to warm his bed and his heart.' The girl removed the bowl of water that she'd placed by Layla's feet. 'You carry a big responsibility.'

The words did nothing to ease the churning in her stomach. Layla knew she'd warm the bed simply by lying in it, but she also knew that wasn't what the girl meant. She did not feel it appropriate to point out the absurdity of being chosen to warm his heart when his heart was in his thoracic cavity and more than capable of maintaining its own temperature. No, what the girl was *really* pointing out was that she was filling the gap left by his wife. Suddenly Layla realised that it was all very well to speak blithely of a different sort of marriage but in the end this union was about a man and a woman spending their lives together, and she had no idea if he would even be able to treat her with civility, given everything that had happened.

But what difference did it make? Her alternative was marriage to Hassan and nothing could be worse.

Rationalising that, Layla only half listened as the girl braided her hair and continued to praise Raz in terms close to hero-worship. She was aware of the worsening throb in her head and the steady gnawing of anxiety about her sister. And beneath all that there was anxiety about herself. About what lay ahead. About *him*.

It was all very well to state bravely that this was what she wanted. Quite another thing to contemplate the reality.

I will inevitably hurt you—as you would know if you'd read the book.

'The book' was safely tucked away in her bag, along with the other book she'd smuggled out of the Citadel. Raz had told her she didn't need to read it but she couldn't think of anything worse than relying entirely on someone else for information.

She wished she could have time alone to study it before the wedding, but there seemed to be no chance of that and she couldn't argue with his decision to proceed as quickly as possible.

Hassan would be out looking for her. *And for Yasmin.*

She winced as the girl's fingers encountered a fresh bruise.

'His Highness told me you fell from your horse. It's a shame that you can't ride because he is a magnificent horseman.'

The implication being that he couldn't have picked a worse match in her.

Her confidence plummeting as each of Raz's qualities was revealed, Layla sank into gloom. She was starting to wonder if this might not have been the worst idea of her life.

And then she heard noise from outside the tent and sat up,

clutching the towel, terrified that Hassan might have found them. 'Who is that?'

'The wedding guests. A Bedouin wedding gives everyone a chance to dress up and celebrate. Word has spread that His Royal Highness Raz Al Zahki is to marry Her Royal Highness Princess Layla of Tazkhan.' There was a brittle note to her tone. 'Even though it is short notice, he wants as many of the local people here as possible. It's important that it is witnessed.'

He wanted rumour spread. He wanted Hassan to hear and be afraid.

'Even when I'm married to Raz Al Zahki, Hassan is unlikely to step aside.'

'His Highness will know what to do.'

Layla was surprised by how much faith people seemed to have in him. She was used to living in an atmosphere of negativity and resentment, not of trust.

Nothing about this new life seemed familiar, and certainly not the dress.

She had never worn anything so beautiful. Her hair, now shiny and clean, was concealed by a veil and her eyes had been accentuated by kohl. The shiny gloss the girl applied to her mouth felt sticky and strange and Layla felt utterly unlike herself.

Any hopes she'd had of being able to sneak a look at the *Kama Sutra* died as she was immediately led outside. It seemed that she and Raz Al Zahki agreed on at least one thing, and that was that the marriage should take place as fast as possible.

And clearly he had also decided that there should be as many witnesses as possible, because a surprising number of people had poured into the desert camp in the time it had taken her to wash and change.

The wedding itself was a blur, conducted with an urgency

driven not by feelings of sentimentality but by the knowledge that any delay could give Hassan an advantage.

Layla kept her gaze focused ahead of her, aware of what felt like a thousand pairs of eyes fixed on her—some curious, others with unconcealed hostility.

And all the time she was aware of Raz next to her, tall and powerful, doing his duty for the good of his people, his own personal wishes set aside.

The event held no emotional meaning for either of them, but they stood side by side, spoke the words required of them, and Layla felt a rush of relief that came from the knowledge that no matter what happened now Hassan couldn't make her his wife.

As Raz turned towards her relief was washed away by reality.

She was now living in the enemy camp with a man who had no reason to feel anything but animosity and contempt for her.

The fact that this was a marriage of expediency didn't seem to bother the guests, who danced and celebrated until Layla was almost dropping with exhaustion.

And he noticed, of course, because it seemed he noticed everything—from the slightest change in the wind's direction to a child who had wandered off unattended.

'Come.'

Just a single word, but delivered with such authority that it didn't occur to her to contradict him. Or maybe it was that she was too preoccupied with what lay ahead.

She hoped the physical side of their relationship didn't require too much input from her because she was fairly sure she was going to fall asleep the moment she lay flat.

They were halfway towards the tent when there was a sound in the distance. She heard horses and shouts and Raz tightened his hand over hers and hauled her close to his side.

Moments later two men she recognised from her arrival at the camp galloped up with the Sheikh's stallion—that same huge black beast that had become as much of a legend as its master.

Layla strained her ears to catch what they were saying and then gasped as firm hands grasped her and swung her onto the back of the animal. Less than thrilled at being back on a horse so soon after her last experience, she clutched at the stallion's mane feeling unbalanced and horribly unsafe.

Moments later Raz vaulted on behind her and locked his arm around her waist.

'I'm sorry to do this to you when you're still bruised after your last encounter with a horse, but Hassan has discovered your absence.' His mouth was right by her ear. 'Right now he is doing everything in his power to find you. It isn't safe to stay. We must move on.'

'But now that we're married—'

'That does not make it safe. No matter what circumstances led to our marriage, you are mine now and I will protect you. You have my word on that.'

Layla heard the steel in his voice and wondered if he were thinking of his wife.

Did he blame himself for not preventing the accident that had killed her?

Had she given him yet more responsibility to add to the load he already carried?

'Could we use a different mode of transport? I'll slow you down. I can't ride.'

'I am the one doing the riding. You are merely the passenger.'

'I'll fall off.' She glanced down and then wished she hadn't. It was a long way to the ground. The stallion was enormous and she felt the power of him beneath her, felt the quivering suppressed energy, and remembered how the horse Yasmin had taken from her father's stables had shot forward like an arrow from a bow, leaving her in an aching heap on the sand.

His arm tightened around her. 'I will *not* let you fall.'

'Can't we use a helicopter or a Jeep or something?'

'One of my men is flying the helicopter and another is taking a Jeep to provide a decoy. They will not expect us to be on horseback. It is the safest way.'

Thinking that he had a very different idea of the definition of 'safe', Layla gripped tightly with her legs and felt the warm flanks of the quivering horse pressing against her bare thighs. 'I'm not dressed for this.'

Even as she said the words a cloak was wrapped around her and he said something to someone close by.

'There is no time to change. You will be fine. Trust me.'

Layla was about to point out that she didn't trust him any more than he trusted her, but the horse sprang forward and she squeezed her eyes shut.

'Is it wise to ride at night?'

'No. Which is why Hassan will not look for us on horseback.'

'Is that supposed to be comforting?' She thought she heard him laugh but decided it must have been the wind, because who could find such a dangerous situation amusing?

'I know this area as well as you know the palace. We are following the stars and the riverbed. Now, relax and go with the rhythm of the horse. You are very tense and that will make the whole thing more uncomfortable.'

Go with the rhythm of the horse…

She told herself that last time she hadn't had a skilled rider in control or a strong male arm wrapped around her.

'Pull the scarf across your mouth.'

She released her rigid grip on the horse's mane to do as he instructed.

She wanted to ask where they were going, but knew the

question was not only superfluous but also potentially haz-
ardous because the hooves of the horses sent sand flying into
the air and she only had a thin layer of scarf protecting her. So
she kept her mouth closed and tried to remember what she'd
read about riding, and then realised it didn't matter because
he knew and was driving the horse forward, controlling the
animal with one hand on the reins while the other remained
firmly locked around her waist.

She was aware of the dull thud of hooves on sand, of the
feel of Raz's thighs pressed hard against hers and the brush
of the cool night air on her face. A sensation tore through her
that she didn't recognise and it took her a few moments to
realise it was exhilaration. With the responsibility for controlling the horse in someone else's hands, the ride on the
back of this powerful animal was the most exciting, breath-
taking experience of her life. In her restricted, regimented
life this was the closest she'd ever come to freedom, and it
felt so good she smiled behind the protective covering of the
scarf. She couldn't remember when she'd last smiled, but
she was smiling now as each pounding stride of the horse
took her further away from Hassan. It felt like the end of
something—and then she remembered that Hassan was unlikely to give up that easily.

And Yasmin was out in the desert alone and lost.

Her smile faded.

She hoped Salem's knowledge of the desert was as good
as it was reputed to be and that he'd find her sister quickly.

They rode for several hours, until time blurred and sleep
overcame her. Several times she was jarred awake as her head
hit his shoulder, and eventually he shifted position to give her
somewhere to rest her head.

'Sleep, Princess.'

And she did, because her body gave her no choice, exhausted by the exertions of the past twenty-four hours. Her

last coherent thought before her brain shut down was that sleeping against his chest like this was the safest she'd felt in her life.

CHAPTER FOUR

SHE WAS SNUGGLED against him, lulled to sleep by the movement of the horse.

The closeness of her disturbed him as much as the realisation that she was nothing like he'd imagined her to be when people had spoken her name. He'd visualised someone pampered and privileged. Someone spoiled and entitled. When he'd first seen her in his tent he'd assumed she was an opportunist, switching sides to protect herself before the inevitable shift in power.

At some point from her arrival in the camp to her falling asleep against him his view on her had become clouded, and now he was forced to admit he didn't know what he was dealing with.

Dawn rose over the desert, and in the distance he saw the familiar shape of trees and tents clustered around the small, lush oasis that marked one of his favourite places on earth.

His heart clenched as it always did when he arrived here.

Perhaps he shouldn't have brought her, but what choice did he have?

Alerted to their presence, people emerged from tents. The rising sun glinted off the dunes and Raz brought his horse to a halt.

'Princess?' He spoke the word softly and she stirred against him, her hand locked on the sleeve of his robe.

Raz looked down at that hand. Her fingers were slender and he realised this was the first time he'd seen any part of her other than her face. 'Layla!' He used her name for the first time and she came awake with a start, her eyes blurred with sleep as she tried to focus and orientate herself.

'I fell asleep?'

'For several hours.' He held the stallion steady and then dismounted in a smooth movement. 'Swing your leg over the saddle and I'll help you down.'

She did it without fuss, but the moment her feet touched the ground she winced and gripped the horse for balance. They'd ridden for hours and she was already aching and bruised from her ride from the Citadel. He knew virtually nothing about her but suspected only dire need would drive her to steady herself against his horse.

The stallion gave a snort of disapproval and threw up its head in disgust.

Raz put his hand on his horse's neck and spoke calmly. 'Your muscles will soon become accustomed to riding.'

'I'm fine, really.'

'You are hoping never to see another horse in your life,' he said dryly, 'but horses are an essential part of my life. I own several stud farms. Two in the US, one in England and one here in Tazkhan.'

'I know. Your aim is to promote the highest standards in breeding. You specialise in endurance and racing. People send mares from all over the world to be covered by your stallions. You rode in the endurance team on your favourite horse, Raja.'

He hid his surprise. 'You know a great deal about my horses.'

'I know nothing about your horses.' This time she was the one to speak in a dry tone. 'But I will try very hard to learn.'

'Is that what you want?'

She hesitated. 'Of course. Although I can't promise I'll show any aptitude. I'm not very coordinated and I'm not sure animals like me much.' Hesitant, she reached out and patted the stallion's neck. 'Is this Raja? I'm incredibly grateful to him for not throwing me off.'

'I bred him. He was sired by my father's stallion.'

'He's beautiful. But big.'

Presumably her legs had steadied because she stepped back and looked around her for the first time.

'Where are we? We can stay with these people? In their homes? Will we be welcome?'

There wasn't a place in the desert where he wasn't welcome, but he didn't say that to her.

'The Bedouin pride themselves on their hospitality. A visitor may stay three days and three nights, after which he is considered sufficiently refreshed to be able to continue his journey.'

'Is that what we're going to do?'

Raz didn't reply. He wasn't used to sharing his plans with anyone, least of all the daughter of the man who had ripped his life into shreds. 'The oasis here is famed for its beauty. You can relax here, knowing you are safe.'

'And my sister?'

'When I have news from Salem I will tell you. And now I have things I must do.'

She didn't ask what things. She simply stared at the red-gold of the dunes as they rose against the sunrise as if she were seeing the desert for the first time, while Raz found himself looking at her profile. She had to be exhausted and in pain after the long ride, but she hadn't once complained.

He wondered what she was thinking.

Was she still relieved not to have married Hassan?

Was she nervous? Regretting her decision to marry a man she didn't know?

On impulse he reached out to touch her shoulder, and then changed his mind and withdrew his hand. 'The waters of the oasis are good for muscle ache.'

'I'll remember that, thank you.'

A young woman emerged from one of the tents and Raz felt a sudden rush of tension. In an ideal world he would have prepared for this encounter with more care, but the world was rarely ideal.

'This is Nadia. If there is anything you need she will help you.'

Nadia looked from him to Layla, unable to hide her dismay. 'So it's true? You married her?'

Her voice shook and Raz shot her a warning look.

'Yes. And you will make her welcome.'

For a moment he thought she was going to refuse.

Their eyes met and suddenly he wondered whether her feelings about this development were more complicated than he'd imagined.

Nadia's breathing was shallow, but she gave a brief nod. 'Of course. Come this way, Your Highness.' The correct mode of address was spoken through clenched teeth, but Raz decided to overlook that for now.

His sudden marriage would have come as a massive shock to Nadia. It was fair that she be given time to adjust.

Raz saw Layla glance towards him and wondered if the other girl's open hostility had upset her.

Or perhaps she was suddenly realising that this marriage was real.

Out of the frying pan into the fire?

'Bathe, eat, rest,' he told her quietly, 'and I will see you later.'

Bathe, eat, rest.

All of it seemed to be leading to one thing. The night.

I will see you later.

Layla tried not to think about it. It was something to be done, that was all. She would endure it as she had endured the long gallop on the horse and a thousand other discomforts in her life. Really, how bad could it be?

'His Highness gave instructions that you are to swim. He says it will ease the pain in your muscles.' Nadia was barely civil as she led her towards the tents, but Layla was starting to get used to that attitude from everyone close to the Sheikh.

She felt as welcome as a scorpion in the heel of someone's boot.

All the same, she wondered what the other girl's relationship was with him. She'd seen the look they'd exchanged and it had been obvious to her that they knew each other well.

She wondered if the woman had been his lover, but told herself she had no reason to mind even if she had.

Baking hot under the desert sun, Layla removed her cloak. Nadia turned pale.

'Where did you get that dress?'

Layla glanced down at herself and noticed that the silk was discoloured by sand and dust from the ride. 'I was given it. Why?'

'No reason.' Nadia's lips were bloodless. 'I will leave towels on the rocks, Your Highness, and lay out clean clothes in the tent for you to change into when you have finished.'

'I can't swim,' Layla admitted. 'Is the oasis deep?'

Nadia led her along a narrow path. 'Not if you enter the pool by the rocks on the far side.'

The rocks on the far side.

Layla committed that to memory because she didn't want to get it wrong.

Nothing about her first glimpse of the camp had prepared her for the beauty of the oasis. Shaded by date palms, the still pool of water looked temptingly cool after the long, dusty ride.

This part of the pool was secluded, the view from the

other tents obscured by palms and citrus trees. Just one tent stood close by and Nadia gestured with her head. 'That is His Highness's tent. I will leave clothes there and put food in the tent. If you need anything, just call, but the pool is safe in the daytime. I'll go and fetch towels.'

Layla didn't ask what happened at night. She was too busy wondering who had given up their tent for the Sheikh.

It was obvious it had prime position, set apart from the others and opening onto what effectively became a private pool.

But not *that* private.

Layla glanced around her, aware that anyone could walk past at any time.

Having only ever undressed behind a locked door, she decided to keep her dress on. It was ruined anyway, so she might as well get one last use out of it.

Removing the belt, she walked to the rocks at the far side of the pool, as Nadia had instructed, and slid into the water.

Stretching out her legs, she felt for the bottom with her feet—but there was no bottom.

Too late, she realised how deep it was and clung tightly to the slippery rock with her fingers, trying to pull herself out again. Just as the thought flashed into her head that Nadia had deliberately sent her to deep water she sank under the surface, dragged down by the weight of the saturated dress.

Trying not to panic, Layla attempted to haul herself up, but her fingers slipped and she sank under the surface, choking.

Water flooded through her mouth and her ears and she kicked hard, but the dress wrapped itself around her ankles, pulling her down.

Just when she'd thought there was no way she was ever going to get out of this alive she felt a disturbance in the water next to her and strong hands hauled her upwards, towards the light. Layla broke the surface of the water, gasping and coughing.

'Are you trying to drown yourself?' His black hair plastered to his head, Raz lifted her onto the rocks and then launched himself out of the water next to her, water streaming from the gleaming, pumped muscles of his bare chest. 'What were you thinking, swimming in a dress?'

Layla couldn't answer. She was too busy coughing and trying not to be sick.

Cursing softly under his breath, he smoothed her soaked hair away from her face. 'You are all right now. You are safe. It was lucky I decided to come back and check on you.'

'I went under—'

'Because you chose to swim in your dress,' he breathed, and she shook her head.

'I never intended to swim. I can't swim. I was just going to dip myself in the water.'

'Fully clothed?'

It sounded ridiculous, spelled out like that, and her face turned fiery hot. 'I thought someone might walk along and see me. The dress was ruined anyway so I thought I'd just keep it on and paddle.'

'In the deepest end of the pool?'

'I thought it was the shallow end.' Layla glanced up at him, puzzled, and saw his eyes darken dangerously.

'Why would you think that? Who told you it was the shallow end?'

She wasn't going to tell him that when there was already friction. 'It was my fault,' Layla muttered 'I should have checked for myself.'

Without speaking, he unfastened the back of her dress. 'Take this off. Go to the other end of the pool where the water is only waist deep. You will be safe and undisturbed, I promise.'

'Where are you going?'

'There is a conversation I need to have and it would seem

that it can't wait.' His voice vibrating with anger, he vaulted to his feet and strode back towards the tent.

Moments later Layla heard his voice and winced, because it was obvious to her that however much Nadia had loathed her before this, she was going to loathe her a thousand times more by the time Raz had finished ripping strips from her in that icy voice of his. She thought she heard muffled sobs and closed her eyes, because the whole situation was turning into a complex mess and without the facts she had no idea how she was supposed to handle it.

Taking refuge in the practical, she peeled off the soaked dress and forced herself back into the water again—more because she didn't want to let fear beat her than because she wanted to wash. This time she was relieved to feel the bottom under her feet. As he had promised, the water only reached her waist and she washed herself quickly, still shocked by how close she'd come to drowning in this beautiful place.

The sun sent sparkles of light dancing over the still surface of the pool. Somewhere nearby she heard children playing, their laughter cutting through the stillness of the baking hot air, and the sound surprised her because she hadn't expected to hear children.

She couldn't think of the time she'd last heard children laugh like that. It reminded her of when Yasmin had been very young and Layla had been constantly putting her hand over her mouth to stifle her giggles in case the sound drew unwanted attention. But here no one was trying to muffle the sound and the children played happily, unrestricted.

Thinking of her sister brought a lump to her throat.

Where was she now?

If only she were at least alive, Layla would never complain about anything ever again.

Listening to the children, she was tempted to go and watch them, but then decided she'd encountered enough hostility for one day. Instead she wrapped herself in the towels that had been left for her and walked the short distance to the tent, hoping that Nadia wouldn't be there.

Stepping inside, she stopped in surprise.

She'd expected something basic, but this tent was not only fully furnished but luxurious, decorated in rich reds and deep purples. There was a seating area piled with soft cushions and a low bed covered in silk sheets, with a thick cover for cold desert nights.

It was idyllic.

It was—Layla swallowed hard—*it was romantic.*

Someone had laid food on a low table near to the door, but Layla wasn't hungry. She couldn't even think about food after everything that had happened. Did Nadia really hate her so much she would want her dead? And what had Raz said to her that had caused her such distress?

Feeling sick from nerves and oasis water, she pulled on the clothes and sank onto the cushions.

Despite worry about Nadia, and anxiety for her sister, her mind was dominated by thoughts of the night ahead.

She would have spent the day reading, but her books had been left behind at the first camp so she had nothing but her imagination to occupy her time, and by the time Raz finally appeared she was so worked up she jumped out of her skin.

'You startled me.'

His gaze rested on the untouched food and a faint frown touched his forehead. 'You haven't touched the food. Are you unwell after the incident earlier?'

'No. I just wasn't hungry.'

'If you do not eat you will make yourself ill.'

She didn't tell him that she already felt ill. That nerves had created an uncomfortable lump in her stomach, leaving no room for food. 'I won't be ill. I'm very fit.'

'But you can't swim?'

'There is nowhere to swim in the palace so I've never had opportunity.'

'Then that's something we must fix.' A ghost of a smile touched his mouth. 'Swimming in the oasis is one of life's pleasures.'

Her heart was pumping so fast she worried she was going to pass out, and when he took her hand and drew her towards him she stopped breathing.

'I am sorry for what happened to you.'

'Is Nadia—?'

'I don't want to talk about Nadia. She has no relevance to what is happening between us and I've dealt with her. Now you need to relax.' His voice soft, he smoothed her hair back from her face. 'You are very tense and there is no need to be.'

Behind him, through the crack in the tent, she could see the sun turning dark red as it set and it shocked her because she hadn't realised it was so late.

'I'm not tense.'

'Yes, you are, and that is hardly surprising.' His fingers lingered in her hair. 'This is not how you dreamed your wedding night would be, I'm sure.'

'I never dreamed about it. I'm not a dreamy person, Your Highness.'

'Raz.' He let a strand of her hair twist itself around his fingers, frowning as she flinched away from him. 'You don't have to be afraid of me.'

It wasn't fear that made her stomach cramp, but she wasn't sure what it was because it was a feeling she didn't recognise.

All she knew was that she'd never felt more uncomfortable in her life. He clearly thought she'd spent her formative years dreaming of weddings and happy endings whereas nothing could have been further from the truth.

'I am not a romantic person,' she reminded him. 'I thought

I'd made that clear. I hope that won't be a problem. I assumed you wouldn't want that.'

What if he did?

Perhaps he was expecting her to fall instantly in love with him and she knew that was never going to happen.

The heat in the tent was stifling and he was standing close to her. *So close she could feel the heat and power of him.* The breath was locked in her throat and Layla had no idea what she was supposed to do next. Was he expecting her to kiss him? Was he supposed to go first or was she? Both together?

Layla desperately wished she'd had time to study the various options.

She wished she'd read *that* book long before now, instead of grabbing it as an afterthought on the run from the palace and her old life.

The gaps in her knowledge were glaringly obvious. For a start, she was confused by how long he'd stood there just looking at her. She'd assumed it would all be over quickly. Instead he seemed to be taking his time. His hand had migrated from her hair to her cheek and the slow, exploratory stroke of his fingers unsettled her.

Her tummy tightened into a knot and her pulse leaped and pounded.

She wanted to look away but his gaze drew her to him, holding her eyes with his. And then his eyes flickered to her mouth and that made her feel strange, too. As did his next words.

'So what *did* you dream about when you were growing up in the palace?'

How was she supposed to answer that? Every day had been focused on survival. On protecting her sister. 'I didn't really dream. I prefer to focus on things that are real. Tangible.'

'You had no wish for the future?'

'If I did then it was a hope that the future would be better than the present.' She saw him frown slightly and felt his thumb slide slowly over the line of her jaw.

'The present was hard for you?'

What could she say? However hard it had been for her, she knew it must have been so much harder for him. He'd lost his father and the woman he'd loved. 'I had my sister.'

A faint smile touched the corner of his mouth. 'You're being evasive, but I'll overlook it for now because the past has no place in our bedroom.'

Our bedroom.

Her heart was pounding furiously and she found herself trapped by his dark gaze as he slid his hands into her hair and tilted her face to his.

'If I do anything you don't like you must tell me,' he breathed.

She'd just had time to think that was a very strange thing to say, because she had no expectation of liking any of it, when he lowered his head.

Anticipation held her rigid.

That sensuously curved mouth hovered close to hers, prolonging the moment of contact. Just as Layla was beginning to wonder whether there was a reason he was taking so long, whether there was something she was supposed to be doing that she wasn't, he slanted his mouth over hers and kissed her.

The gentleness threw her. Braced for something quite different, she found the slow, deliberate movement of his lips on hers shocking. Equally unexpected was the sudden tightening of her stomach and the warmth that rushed through her body and into her limbs. The feelings intensified but still his mouth moved over hers while his hands, buried in her hair, held her head trapped.

She felt his tongue trace the seam of her mouth, teasing, coaxing, and she parted her lips, shocked to feel his tongue delve into her mouth.

Something—*nerves?*—made her shaky? and she closed her hands over his arms to steady herself, her fingers moving over the solid muscle of his biceps. His physical power was undeniable, and she remembered the way he'd controlled the stallion and lifted her out of the pool. But he used that strength lightly now, his hands gentle as he smoothed her hair away from her face and kissed her mouth, all the time watching her through slumbrous dark eyes that made her aware of every part of herself.

Layla had never felt anything like this before, and she felt a flash of panic because she was a person who liked to understand things and rationalise them. But there was no understanding the searing heat that shot through her body and pooled low in her belly.

Releasing her head, he curved one arm around her back, slid the other around her waist and pulled her into him. She felt the strength and power of his thighs and the hardness of him. Pressed against the evidence of his masculinity, she discovered that the works of Michaelangelo didn't tell the whole story.

Layla was confused by the torrent of sensation that flooded her skin and seeped into her nerve-endings.

'Kiss me back.'

His husky command was spoken against her lips and she stared up at him, unable to see him properly in the darkness but knowing her mouth was just a shadow away from the dangerous curve of his.

Kiss me back.

Wishing she had more knowledge of technique, Layla tentatively touched her lips to his. She wanted to ask, *Is this right?* But then she felt his arm tighten around her waist, drawing her closer. Pressed this close to him, she felt hot and unbalanced in every way. She knew her cheeks were flushed, knew he could taste her confusion on her lips, but still he kissed her and the slowness of it, together with the long drawn-out ache of anticipation and something else she couldn't name, was agonising.

He kissed her until their surroundings faded and the only thing in her vision was him, and then he lifted her in his arms and carried her to the bed. The practical side of her prompted her to tell him she was capable of walking, but she thought it might be a lie so she kept silent and wondered how nerves could weaken limbs.

The light in the tent was dim, but not so dim she couldn't see his face, and she remembered Yasmin dreamily telling her how handsome he was—how he was *'hot'*. At the time Layla hadn't understood how a word used to describe temperature could be used as a positive indicator of visual appeal, but now she realised that looking at him made her *feel* hot. Burning hot. Her skin, her lips and other more sensitive parts of her that she rarely had reason to think about. And while he was kissing her he extracted her from her clothing. The ease with which he accomplished that feat was almost as embarrassing as being naked in front of him.

Grateful for the semi-darkness, she somehow resisted the desperate urge to cover herself. Never in her life had she felt so out of her depth and inadequate, and she lay there, her breathing shallow, staring up at him as he wrenched off his shirt, all the time watching her with eyes almost black in the candlelight.

Layla held her breath because even she, with her limited experience and previously limited interest in the masculine form, could see that his was perfectly proportioned.

Unable to help herself, she let her gaze slide over bronzed, muscular shoulders, down over his chest with its haze of dark hair, and lower still to his board-flat abdomen. She didn't look lower and he slid his fingers under her chin and lifted her face, forcing her to look at him.

'You're scared.'

'No.' Her voice was a whisper. 'But I wish I'd read more.'

'Not all the answers can be found in books.' His thumb brushed the corner of her mouth and his fingers slid into her hair, cupping the back of her head. 'Perhaps you know more than you think you do. Follow your instincts.'

As he drew her head down to his she wanted to tell him that she didn't have any instincts when it came to men, but her tongue wouldn't form the words. Instead it tangled with his, and she heard herself moan into the heat of his clever mouth.

And she discovered she *did* have instincts, because it was instinct that had her sliding her hands into his hair, clutching his head, meeting his hot, seductive kisses with her own. And instinct had her pressing herself closer to him. Later, she'd wonder how a kiss involving her lips could have an effect on her whole body, but right then she wasn't capable of wondering about anything except what was going to happen next.

'Next' was his mouth on her neck—slow, lingering, as everything he did was slow and lingering—and she lay still, hardly breathing as the warmth of his tongue traced the line of her shoulder and moved lower, to her bare breasts.

Her nipples were standing erect and she watched in tense fascination as he paused with his mouth close to that sensitive part of her. She felt the warmth of his breath brush over her skin, followed by the slow, deliberate flick of his tongue as he skilfully teased and toyed with that part of her that had never been touched before. Sensation shot right through her, pooling in her pelvis, until she found it almost impossible to keep still, until the urge to cry out was so powerful she had to bite her lip to stay silent. And what he did to one nipple he did to the other, and when he finally lifted his head and looked at her she found it impossible to look away.

For a moment they stared at each other.

There was a hardness in his eyes, a coldness she wished

she hadn't seen, and then he leaned across the bed and blew out the candle, sending the tent into darkness.

She could no longer see, but she could feel, and the feelings became more acute because everything was focused on that one sense—touch.

The warmth of his palm rested low on her abdomen and she wondered if he knew how much she was aching, just how badly she needed—needed *something*. But of course he knew. She remembered Yasmin's breathless statement that he was supposed to be a skilled lover and knew now that it was true.

No wonder he hadn't bothered returning her book.

I will teach you everything you need to know.

The fact that he knew her body better than she did embarrassed her, but nowhere near as much as when he gently spread her thighs and shifted lower on the bed.

Shocked, and feeling intensely vulnerable, Layla gave a soft gasp as his hand moved with sure, leisurely ease over her abdomen and lower still. He took his time, but whether that was out of respect for her inexperience, patience or just a maddening ability to know how to ramp up the tension until she was at screaming pitch, she didn't know. All she knew was that she was moving her pelvis against his hand, and then his fingers were there, sliding skilfully over that part of her, exploring her with slow, knowing strokes of strong, clever fingers, until her breathing was shallow and her hands fisted in the sheets.

She hadn't known it was possible to feel this.

She couldn't see his face, couldn't see anything except darkness, and that darkness intensified feeling because she never knew what was coming next. She felt him shift above her, then move lower, and this time he put his mouth on her *there*. Shock rocketed through her and her hands moved to push him away, but he caught both her wrists in one hand and held her securely, so that all she could do was lie there and let him do exactly what he wanted to do. And what he did was sinfully good, and he did it again and again, until her body quivered and heated, until she was slippery wet and sensitive, embarrassment blown away by sensation. And with each erotic slide of his tongue the feelings intensified, until the heat of it was so maddening she thought she'd explode.

She knew there was something more, that her body was trying to reach something, somewhere, and she squirmed and shifted, trying to relieve the unfamiliar feelings, and then he shifted position in a lithe movement and came over her, his hand under her bottom.

'I will try not to hurt you...'

His voice was husky and he slid his hand down her thigh, encouraging her to wind her legs across his back. Like this, she was open to him and she was once again grateful for the darkness as she felt the silken power of him against her and the warmth of his breath against her mouth as he lowered his head to kiss her again.

He licked at her lips, kissing her gently as he stayed still, letting her grow used to the feel of him against her. It was shockingly intimate with her legs wrapped around him, and for endless moments he held himself still. Then he eased forward and entered her slowly, gently, holding himself in check with ruthless control, taking it so slowly that the discomfort seemed minimal in comparison to the building frustration. Pain and pleasure mingled. Layla felt herself clench around the hard thickness of him, felt the heat and power of him stretching her, and when his hand tightened on her bottom she lifted herself against him and heard a low sound rumble in his throat as he sheathed himself deep. Her breath caught. The intimacy of it shocked her and she curled her fingers over his biceps and then up to his shoulders, aware that he was holding himself still and knowing that he did it for her.

'Are you all right?'

His voice was low and very male, and she opened her eyes, even though she couldn't see him, and said yes, even though she wasn't sure it was true.

She wasn't all right. With him so deeply inside her she felt shaken and unbalanced, as out of her depth as she had in the pool. Only this time instead of drowning in water she was drowning in sensation.

She didn't know what was happening, but she knew she wanted this, *needed* this, and when he lowered his mouth to hers and kissed her she kissed him back, her tongue tangling with his.

He eased back slightly and then moved into her again. She felt her body yield against the male thickness of him, discovered that if she relaxed it was easier, that when he shifted his angle the pleasure intensified and poured through her in long, wicked waves of ecstasy. He was deep, deep inside her, his hand locked in her hair as he controlled the rhythm, all the time kissing her. And she recognised nothing that was happening to her body, *knew* nothing—but he did, and he used that skill and experience to drive her higher and higher, until something strange happened, something unfamiliar and intensely exciting, until screaming ecstasy exploded into an almost unbearable shower of sensation that made her cry out despite her attempts to stay silent.

He trapped the sound with his mouth, kissing her through it as she felt her body tighten around the smooth, hard length of him. She felt the sudden tension of his shoulders under her fingers and then heard him groan deep in his throat as her body drove his over the edge. It was the most thrilling, explosive, intense experience of her life and afterwards Layla lay still, crushed by the weight of him and the knowledge that she had lived with herself for twenty-three years and yet not known herself at all.

She'd had no idea she was even capable of feeling that way.

Her illusions about herself had disintegrated. She'd never thought of herself as romantic, nor particularly physical. Nothing in her past had prepared her for what she'd just experienced. And she realised that delving into a book for information wouldn't have made a difference, because there were no words that could adequately describe what she'd just experienced.

Nothing she'd read could have prepared her for pleasure.

Shattered by the experience, her expectations blown apart, Layla lay there, not knowing what words were appropriate. They'd shared the ultimate intimacy and yet outside the silken haven of his bed they were strangers.

She lay rigid, feeling as if she should say something, trying out various sentences in her head. But before she could utter any of them she felt him rise from the bed. Her burning skin chilled instantly and that chill spread through her bones as rapidly as the heat had done.

Shattered and confused, Layla lay still in the darkness, listening as he dressed. Was this normal?

Was it usual for a man to stand up and leave the bed afterwards?

Or did his response have something to do with his wife?

Was that why he'd blown out the candle? Had he been imagining that he was with someone else? Or was it that he couldn't bear to look at her?

It sounded as if he were going to stride out of the tent without looking back, but then he paused, his hand on the heavy fabric that protected them from the heat of the sun and the cold of the night. Moonlight shone through the slit in the tent and in that moment Layla saw him. Saw the hard, savage lines of his handsome face and the emptiness in those cold eyes that were as black as a starless night.

She stared at him in silence, trying to read him, trying to understand what was going on and failing.

She had no idea what that look meant. No idea what was going through his head.

And now she wished she'd kept her eyes closed. Pretended to be asleep. Anything, to avoid a situation in which she was clueless.

Should she speak?

Was he waiting for her to say something?

And then, before she could decide whether to speak or not, he turned and strode out of the tent, leaving her alone.

CHAPTER FIVE

HE RODE RAJA deep into the desert, trying to escape the weight of his feelings but failing, because wherever he went they followed. His mouth was dry with the bitter taste of betrayal, the past a deep ache inside him that wouldn't heal.

There were so many issues demanding his attention, but the only thing on his mind was Layla.

He'd felt nothing but contempt for her family for so long that when she'd arrived in his camp and offered herself to him he'd treated her proposal with suspicion. Even when it had become clear to him that her life had been very different from the one he'd imagined for her, his feelings towards her hadn't warmed.

But now?

The scent of her clung to his skin and her soft gasps echoed around his head, refusing to be silenced by his own vicious conflict.

As if sensing his tension, the horse under him stamped impatiently. Raz soothed him gently with his hands and his voice until Raja calmed and stood still.

He had a sudden vision of Layla smuggling the *Kama Sutra* from her father's library before leaving the only home she'd ever known. He thought of her climbing onto a horse, even though she didn't ride, and then going in search of him even though she knew exactly how she felt about her family.

And then he thought about her standing still and straight next to him, speaking her vows in the hope that the union would ensure the safety of her sister, and writhing under his hands as he'd shown her what her body could do.

The thought of it sent heat rushing through him and he cursed softly.

He told himself that respect and powerful sexual chemistry didn't change the fact he wasn't ready to feel anything for another woman. Nor did it change the fact that he didn't want her feeling anything for him.

Nothing changed the fact that this marriage politically motivated.

Was she all she seemed to be, or was she a clever opportunist who had the sense to change sides for her own protection?

His suspicions were deep-set, rooted in a lifetime of bitter feud.

So why did the knowledge that he'd hurt her rub at his nerves like sand wedged in his boot?

Staring at the sunrise, he told himself it was a good thing.

He told himself that anger was a thousand times safer than those softer emotions that could fell a man faster than a samurai sword.

'Your Highness.'

It was Abdul, never far from his side and as much a father to him as his own had been.

'You should not be out here alone.'

'I don't appear to *be* alone.'

Ignoring the irony in his voice, Abdul touched his arm. 'This is hard for you, but you did the right thing marrying her.'

'Did I?' He heard the harshness in his own voice and winced, because he wasn't in the habit of revealing his weaknesses to those around him. 'We need to keep an eye on Nadia.'

'Yes. I can imagine she is very upset. But no doubt Her Highness will deal with that sensitively. She seems like a very sensible young woman.'

Sensible? Raz could have agreed with him, but he knew it wasn't her logic or her ordered thought-processes that teased and tormented his brain.

It was something far more intimate and a thousand times more dangerous.

Layla awoke slowly, aware of the sounds of animals, the laughter of children, the hum of voices. None of them belonged to Raz.

The side of the bed where he would have slept was cold, the pillow smooth and untouched.

Her body ached from her night with him, making it impossible to blot it out or forget.

He'd come to her in darkness and then he'd walked away.

Had he known how his touch had made her feel?

Of course he had. His expertise had never been in question. From the first touch to the last, he'd known exactly what he was doing to her.

Layla rolled onto her back and stared up at the roof of the tent.

But as for the rest of it—as for how she felt inside and in her head...

How could he understand that when she didn't understand it herself?

She'd thought she knew herself very well but it turned out she didn't know herself at all, because she hadn't known she was capable of feeling like *that*.

Sheltered by the silk sheets, she slid her hand over her breasts, still tender from the touch of his mouth and the roughness of his jaw. He'd touched her *there* and then he'd—

'Your Highness?' Nadia stood in the entrance to the tent,

her expression frozen as she saw the clothes piled on the floor. 'I have instructions to help you dress and fetch you anything you need.'

What did she need?

Layla had no idea. She felt like a jigsaw someone had dropped. She had no idea how to fit the pieces back together because she no longer recognised the picture. And she had no idea how to make peace with Nadia. It didn't feel good to watch the other woman's pain and know she was somehow the cause.

It was the first time they'd seen each other since the incident in the pool, but Layla decided that Raz had already said whatever needed to be said so didn't raise the topic.

'There is nothing I need, thank you.' She watched as Nadia moved around the tent, placing food on the rug and laying out fresh clothes. She wanted to ask where Raz was, but didn't want to reveal how much she minded his absence—especially not to this girl, who clearly resented Layla's presence and wished she were anywhere but there.

Layla wondered again if she were in love with Raz herself. Was that the reason for the rigid expression and the fact she didn't meet her eyes? Or was it because of who Layla was?

In the end concern for him overruled pride.

'Have you seen His Highness?'

Nadia paused in the entrance of the tent. 'The rumour is that he has gone to find Hassan and talk to him. If he is killed it will be *your* fault.'

The girl blurted out the words and then left the tent, leaving Layla alone with nothing but her conscience to keep her company.

The news that he'd gone to find Hassan disturbed her—not because she underestimated Raz's strength, but because she knew just how duplicitous Hassan could be. He was neither honest nor honourable, and she knew better than most that he was at his most dangerous when he was cornered.

Should she have voiced her suspicions to Raz?

Weighed down by her worry, the hours dragged past. Without access to the library Layla had nothing to distract her from her thoughts, no hope of reaching a state of relaxation. She would have loved to talk to someone but no one came near her. Even Nadia stayed away, and Layla realised that when she'd suggested this marriage she'd given no consideration to how others would feel about it.

Did they all think she'd put Raz at risk?

What if Nadia was right and by coming to him she'd created trouble?

What if Hassan found them here?

It felt like the longest day of her life, and she spent most of it alone, sitting by the oasis, aware of the unfamiliar soreness and aching in her body.

Several times she heard children laughing and the sound reminded her so much of her sister that a lump wedged itself in her throat. Where was she? Had Salem found her? Was she in trouble? *Dead?*

If Hassan had found her before Salem then the chances were she was already in America.

As darkness fell the noise of chatter faded, leaving only the sounds of the desert at night.

Layla lay still on the bed, staring at the single candle that had been lit for her, so tense she could hear her own breathing in the silence of the tent.

Would he come?

Would it be like the night before?

The question swirled around in her head until eventually she fell asleep. When she woke it was light, his side of the bed was still cold, and she had her answer.

He hadn't come.

She was still alone in the bed and she had no idea if Raz had even returned.

Seriously concerned, she swallowed her pride and sought out Nadia once more.

'I do not know where he is, Your Highness.' Her voice was frosty and hovered on the edge of rude. 'He never reveals his plans. And now he's brought you here the risk to him personally will be even greater.'

With no hard evidence with which to refute that challenge, Layla bowed out of the conversation. Guilt gnawed at her, driven by anxiety that Nadia could be right. Had she increased his problems? Had she made things worse, not better?

Or did his unexplained absence have nothing to do with Hassan?

What if it were driven by something even more personal?

Something to do with the night they'd spent together.

Was he thinking of his wife?

Layla spent a second day alone, with only her imagination for company, and was beginning another night the same way when she heard the sound of horses and knew it was him.

The rush of relief was quickly followed by other, more complex feelings.

All day she'd wanted to see him, but now he was here she wished she were on her own again. She had no idea what to say or what to do. She was hardly in a position to play the role of concerned wife, but still she *was* concerned.

Embarrassed, uncomfortable, and burning hot at the thought of the night before them, Layla sat rigid, wishing that there was a rulebook she could follow, an instruction manual—*anything* that might give her clues about how she was supposed to behave.

She heard his voice, deep and instantly recognizable, as he responded to people around him, but still he didn't appear in the tent. It seemed he had time for everyone except her.

Or maybe he was once again waiting for darkness. Maybe he just couldn't face looking at her.

As that explanation occurred to her embarrassment turned to humiliation.

Everyone would know the Sheikh had stayed away from his new bride.

That indisputable fact was a stark reminder that physical intimacy didn't mean emotional intimacy.

Curled up in a ball under the covers, Layla felt more alone than she ever had in her life.

At least back in the Citadel she'd had Yasmin. Her life had been wretched, but familiar. She'd known the rules, known what was expected of her and been able to rationalise every one of her thoughts and feelings.

Here, she was totally isolated, living with a man who apparently loathed her so deeply he couldn't bear to set eyes on her, tormented by emotions and feelings that were totally unfamiliar.

She heard a splash from nearby and assumed he'd gone for a swim in the oasis.

The fact that he hadn't even greeted her first upset her more than she could rationalise. She shouldn't care, should she? She wasn't *allowed* to care.

Layla hesitated for a moment, but then slid quietly out of the bed and peeped through the slit in the tent. It was dark, but without the pollution of the city there was sufficient light for her to make out powerful shoulders as he swam.

She stared at those bare, powerful shoulders, fascinated and shocked in equal amounts. If anyone had told her days ago she'd be hiding in a tent in the hope of getting a glimpse of a naked man she would have laughed at them. But this wasn't any naked man, of course. This was Raz. And because he'd blown out the candles she had yet to see his body.

And she couldn't really see it now—just the occasional

tantalising hint of male muscle and power as he swam with smooth, steady movements.

He reached the far side of the pool and turned. Layla shot back into bed, terrified of being caught.

By the time he walked into the tent she was safely under the covers with her eyes closed.

She heard his soft tread, then silence, and she knew he was looking at her although surely the lack of light would restrict his vision.

Feeling as if someone had set fire to her, Layla kept her eyes closed and tried to breathe evenly. She stayed completely still. Even when the mattress moved under his weight she didn't move.

She lay rigid, churned up inside by his reappearance, shocked that he'd stayed away for two days and then not even greeted her on his return, and shocked that such an action on his part could hurt so badly.

'A tip for the future. No one is that tense when they sleep.'

His voice was deep and soft and she turned, giving up the pretence. *What was the point?*

She saw that he had lit a single candle. Not much, but enough to send a golden shadow of light across the bed. *Enough for her to see his face.*

'Where have you been?'

Shock flared in his eyes. 'I'm not in the habit of disclosing my plans to anyone—least of all to a woman I met for the first time only three days ago.'

She wanted to point out that it might only have been three days but that he knew her more intimately than anyone, had revealed a part of her she hadn't even known existed, but she realised there were dark depths to him she hadn't begun to uncover.

'Has there been any news of my sister?'

His gaze was shuttered. 'None.'

Just one word but it made her feel sick, and suddenly all the daydreams were blown out of her head and replaced by stark reality. 'That's bad, isn't it? We should have heard something.'

'If she is alive then Salem will find her.'

'If?'

'Do you want false hope? Because I won't give you that. Lies destroy trust and create nothing but confusion. But until we have evidence that something has happened to her I urge you to stay positive. We have to hope she will have found a way to survive.'

'How? Neither of us spent any time in the desert when we were growing up.'

'And yet Tazkhan is ninety-eight percent desert. How can you serve a country when you are ignorant of the life its people lead?'

Thrown off balance by that unexpected attack, Layla sat up, clutching the silk sheet to her neck as she rose to her own defence. 'That is an unfair accusation. You know nothing of the life my sister and I led.'

'You were in a position of power and lived a life of luxury. There must have been something you could have done.'

Luxury? 'There was, and I did it. I came to you.'

Cold black eyes met hers. 'I am supposed to believe that was an altruistic act on your part? How do I know you didn't just have the sense to move to the winning side?'

It was like being slapped.

'If you believe that, why did you marry me?'

'Because your motivation has no impact on my decision. I am doing what is best for Tazkhan. My personal wishes have no part in this.'

'So when we were in bed you had to force yourself to do those things to me?'

His jaw clenched and his eyes narrowed. Two streaks of colour highlighted the hard, savage lines of his cheekbones.

'For a virgin whose first glimpse of a naked man was from behind a curtain, you suddenly have a great deal to say for yourself.'

She had the distinct impression that he was trying to pick a fight, and suspected she knew why. It was logical, wasn't it?

'You're angry,' she said softly, banking down her own feelings to try and understand his. 'You feel guilty and it's making you angry.'

'You know nothing about my feelings, Princess.'

'And you know nothing about *my* feelings, either. I may be inexperienced, and I admit I'm shy, but don't *ever* assume you know what my life has been. The reason my sister and I have no knowledge of the desert is not because we weren't interested but because we were unable to leave the city walls.'

'Did you ever try?'

Her heart was pounding. 'Yes.'

'And what happened?'

Her mouth was dry. The sudden emergence of a memory she'd squashed down brought sweat to her palms. 'There are some aspects of our past neither one of us wishes to revisit. I think we should both accept that and move on.' Her desperate statement earned her a long, questioning look.

'If your sister is in the desert then Salem will find her.'

He blew out the candle, there was a rustle of clothing as he undressed, and then he joined her in the bed.

Rigid with discomfort, heart pounding, Layla shot to the furthest end of the bed and lay still, hardly daring to breathe in case breathing brought her into contact with him. 'You think I came here to guarantee the continuation of some glittering lifestyle you've imagined for me and yet, feeling that way, you still want to share the bed with me?'

'We're married.'

'But you don't trust me.'

'Sharing a bed doesn't require trust, Princess.' Reaching

for her in the darkness, he hauled her against him. 'It simply requires sexual chemistry, and fortunately we have plenty of that.'

Layla wondered if he could feel her shivering. Wondered if he could feel the heat of her skin and the rapid beat of her heart.

She wanted to ask why he had to blow out the candle before he shared a bed with her, but before she could form words his mouth slanted over hers and his hand slid into her hair. As a concession to the desert heat and the sand she'd tied it back, but he freed it instantly and it tumbled down over her shoulders.

She felt his hand, warm and strong against her bare back, as he pressed her down onto the soft mattress and shifted her underneath him. She felt the weight of him, the strength and the power. Felt his lips move over hers in a kiss that created an instant response. It started deep inside her and then exploded outwards.

Intense excitement shimmered over layers of despair.

Was this how their relationship was going to be?

Days where they saw nothing of each other and nights spent in the dark?

Intimate strangers?

She wondered how his kiss could make her melt when her emotions weren't involved and tried to control her response to him, but her nerve-endings were already on fire and the erotic skill of his mouth left her with no choice but to kiss him back.

His mouth closed over her nipple and Layla moaned. Just like before, he used all his skill and knowledge to drive her crazy, until she was hot and desperate. The only difference was that this time she *knew*. This time she knew what was to come. And when he surged into her with sure, deep strokes she climaxed instantly, and again and then again, while he possessed and controlled her totally.

Afterwards Layla lay there, numb. Maybe she should be grateful for the protection of the darkness, but she wasn't. The knowledge that he could only make love to her if it was in the dark hurt her more than she would have thought possible.

She turned her head, plucking up the courage to talk to him about it, but before she could speak she heard a high-pitched cry coming from close by.

Layla sat upright, heart pounding. 'What's that? It sounded like a child.'

And then the screams began.

Raz moved quickly, his hand on the knife he kept strapped to his belt whenever he was in the desert.

The screams sliced through him, ripping his composure into shreds, because he knew who screamed.

His strides fuelled by a primal need to protect, he tore open the entrance of the tent next to his and saw the child sitting upright, eyes staring in terror, forehead glistening with sweat, as she screamed while Nadia stood there helplessly, hopelessly out of her depth.

'I can't get her to stop.'

In seconds he had the child in his arms, folding her tightly. 'What is wrong with her?'

He heard the raw edge to his tone but the girl simply shrugged defensively.

'She's awake but she won't respond to me. It's as if she's having a fit or something.'

He smoothed the child's hair, gazed into those staring eyes and felt an anxiety so acute it slowed his thinking. He prided himself on the speed and accuracy of his decision-making and yet now, when it was so important to get it right, his brain was motionless.

'Her breathing is fast. Her pulse is fast. Get someone medical in here immediately.'

A calm voice came from the entrance to the tent.

'It isn't a fit and she isn't awake.'

He turned his head and saw Layla, dressed only in a thin nightdress, her hair tangled and tousled from his hands. Her gaze was fixed on the child. 'She's having a night terror. My sister had them all the time at the same age. You shouldn't wake her.'

"She's already awake. Her eyes are open.' Nadia's eyes were cold and unfriendly.

Raz ignored her. 'You have seen this before?' Fear made his voice harsh, but Layla seemed calm and unflustered.

'Many times. It's very unsettling to witness, but I can assure you she will remember nothing of it in the morning. Who is closest to her? Who does she know the best?'

Her gaze flickered expectantly to Nadia and Raz drew a deep breath.

'Me.' The confession was dragged from him, because he hadn't yet decided how to broach this topic and this wasn't the way he would have chosen. 'I have the closest relationship with her.'

Was she shocked?

If so, she didn't show it. Nor did she question what that relationship was.

'In that case you should be the one to tuck her back into bed. Snuggle the sheets around her to make her feel safe. Talk to her quietly. It's not what you say that matters, it's the way you say it. You need to hold her securely. Blow out all the candles except one. Darkness helps. When she goes back to sleep, stay with her for about ten minutes. Once she is deeply asleep it's unlikely to happen again.' Having delivered that set of instructions, she looked at Nadia. 'We should leave. The fewer people the better.'

The other girl's expression was stubborn. 'She knows me.'

'It's better that way.' Layla's voice was firm. 'She needs quiet and just one person she trusts.'

'Do as she says.' Raz lowered his voice and eased the child back under the covers. She was quivering and shivering and it broke his heart to see her. His urge to call a doctor was powerful, but for some reason he was inclined to give Layla's suggestion a try, all the while wondering why he was following the advice of a woman he had no reason to trust.

She'd said it was the tone that mattered, so he spoke nonsense, reciting poetry from his childhood, his hand stroking those fragile shoulders until gradually the little girl calmed and relaxed under his fingers.

Her breathing slowed. Her pulse slowed with it. And as hers did so did his.

Her eyes fluttered shut, those eyelashes dark shadows against cheeks swollen by crying.

Raz sat until the change in her breathing told him she was deeply asleep.

His shoulders ached with tension. His head throbbed with it. Responsibility pressed down on him until he felt not as if he had the world on his shoulders but the universe.

Satisfied that she really was asleep, and unlikely to stir, he rose carefully to his feet and left the tent in search of answers.

Nadia was hovering outside, her expression defensive and defiant. 'I could have settled her. You should not have asked *her* advice.'

'How long has this been going on?'

Her hesitation told him everything.

'A while.'

That reluctant admission did nothing to ease his stress levels.

'*Why* wasn't I told?'

'You were away.'

'But everyone knows I wish to be told of anything that affects my daughter.'

'I didn't think it was significant. She doesn't remember it in the morning.'

Holding onto his temper, knowing that he needed time to cool down before he spoke what was on his mind, Raz clenched his jaw and gestured to the tent he'd just left. 'Stay with her.' Ideally he would have stayed himself, but he needed information so he strode back into his own tent and found Layla standing still in the middle of the room, her hands clenched into fists by her sides, stress evident in every rigid line of her body.

She'd lit the candles and the tent was bathed in a soft, gentle light that revealed sheets still rumpled and twisted from the wild heat of their lovemaking.

She turned as he entered the tent and their gazes locked and held.

Awareness rushed between them and sexual tension crackled like static in the air.

Now you're a woman, he thought, and then blocked that out because he knew this was not the time to address the other issues that were piling up.

'Thank you for your help. You knew what was wrong? You called it a night terror?'

'Yes.' Her confidence reassured him, because he was far from convinced he shouldn't have called for medical assistance.

'You have seen it before?'

'Many times.' Her voice was tight, her eyes shadowed by ghosts and darkness. 'My sister Yasmin started having them when she was five and it carried on for over a year. It might have been longer. I don't really remember. Every night, about an hour after she'd fallen asleep, she'd wake screaming, eyes wide open. She seemed to be awake, but she was asleep. The first time it happened I was just like you—I thought she was awake.'

'But she wasn't?'

'No, and it's very unsettling. It took me a while and some research to realise she was actually asleep.'

Of course she would have researched it. He knew virtually nothing about her, but he knew that much. 'And did your research suggest a cause?'

'There is no single cause, but there are different triggers. A fever, extreme tiredness, and—' She licked her lips and turned her head away so that he could no longer see her eyes. 'And stress. Stress can cause it.'

Guilt twisted inside him, because he knew without a doubt that the trigger in this case was very likely to be stress. And he knew the cause of the stress. 'And in your sister's case?'

'It was definitely stress.'

Still she didn't look at him, and he remembered her reaction to their conversation earlier.

You know nothing of the life my sister and I led.

Raz looked at the tension in those slender shoulders and realised he was looking at far more than a reaction to what had just happened in the tent next door. 'What was she stressed about?'

'This isn't about my sister.' She evaded the question. 'This is about the little girl. Has she been through a bad experience?'

How was he supposed to answer that?

The truth lodged somewhere behind his ribs, Raz turned away and paced to the far side of the tent.

It occurred to him that their relationship was already turning into a minefield of things they didn't talk about, issues they didn't address. The complications were endless.

'How did you stop it happening?'

'I couldn't stop it. I could only deal with it. And I tried to make her feel more secure so that she didn't go to bed scared.'

'She was scared?'

They were exploring two parallel lines of conversation and he was aware that she was avoiding his questions as skilfully as he was avoiding hers.

'They say overstimulation of the central nervous system can cause it. The temptation is always to shake them awake, but it's better if they can just go back to sleep.'

'So there was nothing you could do?'

'I tried very hard not to let anything frighten her.'

There are some aspects of our past neither one of us wishes to revisit.

He caught the bleak look in her eyes and realised just as there were layers to him she hadn't even glimpsed, so there were layers to her. And they were dark layers.

How could it be otherwise, growing up with a man like her father?

Only now did it occur to him how little he knew about his new bride.

An uncomfortable feeling spread down his neck and across his shoulders. 'Did she have reason to be frightened?'

'I started sleeping in the room with her. Sometimes that helped.'

'Layla, why was your sister frightened?'

It was only the second time he'd used her name and he saw her still.

Then she turned her back on him and picked up a robe, slipping it on and covering herself, shielding herself from him in every way. 'If you want to deal with the night terrors, the best thing is to talk to her family and find out what is likely to be causing them.' She fastened the robe around her waist. Her hair poured down her back, thick, shiny and as dark as a starless night. 'That shouldn't be a problem as you seem to know her well.'

Was that the second or third time she'd ignored his question about her life in the palace? Every time he raised it she deflected it. And suddenly he knew this relationship was going to be impossible if they shared nothing.

One of them had to make the first move.

'I do know her well. I know her better than anyone.' He had to push the words past his own natural reluctance to confide. 'She's my daughter.'

CHAPTER SIX

'YOUR *DAUGHTER*?' UNPREPARED for that revelation, Layla simply stared at him. 'You have a daughter?'

'She is six years old.'

He had a daughter.

She sank down onto the bed, her legs shaking, racking her brain for the information she had on him and discovering it to be depressingly sparse. 'I—I didn't know. I had no idea.'

She muttered the words to herself, examining this further piece of evidence to support her suspicion that it was possible to be intimate with someone and yet still know nothing about them.

It didn't make any difference that she'd shared something with him she'd never shared with anyone else. He was still a stranger.

'There are few who know, and those who do know better than to speak of it.'

His voice was flat and she looked at him blankly, shocked into silence and shaken by the enormity of it.

'Why don't people speak of it? Why would you hide the fact that you have a child?'

'I lost my father. I lost my wife—' He didn't finish the sentence. He didn't need to.

Layla knew her face matched the colour of his.

'No.' She shook her head in instinctive denial of that hypothesis. 'That wouldn't have happened.'

'How can you be sure?' His tone was raw. 'You insist on having evidence for everything—show me the evidence that my daughter would have been safe. Did your father live by a code of honour? Did he have boundaries beyond which he wouldn't go? If so, then please enlighten me, because I have seen nothing like that in my dealings with him.'

The shame of it covered her like a filthy, dark sludge. She wanted to dive into the oasis and scrub her skin clean. 'I can't show you evidence. I understand why you kept your daughter's existence a secret. But when I suggested marriage I would have thought—'

'What would you have thought? That I would have confided in you? You arrived in the desert out of nowhere. I married you because I saw the sense in what you proposed but let's not pretend that this marriage is a union of trust.'

His words shook her because in her head she'd started to spin a different scenario. When she looked at him all she could see was the burning heat in his eyes and all she could think of was his body, hard and hot against hers. Out of bed they were strangers but *in* bed? In bed they were as close as it was possible for two people to be and what they did in bed had started to dominate her brain. The craving inside her had intensified to the point that she found herself wishing the daylight hours away because at night there was a chance they'd be together. She found herself hoping desperately for the dark because it was only in the dark that he came to her. Swept away by the darkness and the wildness of the passion she'd started to imagine that this was real but now she realised she'd been deluding herself.

'That is all true, but I am your wife now and that also makes me—'

'Do not say the words.' His voice was thickened with emotion. 'Do not even think of yourself as my daughter's mother.'

The words slid under her ribs like a blade.

She tried to ignore the sharp pain that made it difficult to breathe. Used logic to remind herself that his response was understandable in the circumstances.

The fact that he would kiss her, touch her, didn't mean he trusted her with his daughter.

And she really couldn't blame him for that, could she?

Right now he was the powerful protector, ready to shield his daughter from any threat, and it was clear he considered that threat to be her.

Feeling his struggle to suppress the emotion that threatened to overwhelm him, Layla groped for the best way to handle the situation. 'At least tell me her name.'

'Her name is Zahra.'

'That's a pretty name. Does she know you have married me?'

'No.' He was brutally frank. Everything about him was designed to repel her gentle attempts to ease closer. 'There is no easy way to tell a child I have married the daughter of the man responsible for the death of her mother.'

The knife in her ribs twisted. 'Had I known you had a daughter I never would have suggested this marriage. I had no idea there was a child involved. It changes everything.'

'It changes nothing. This marriage was never personal so what difference would it have made?'

'I would not have sacrificed your daughter's happiness for—'

'For the future of Tazkhan? And what about your sister's safety? What about your own marriage to Hassan? Because that's why you came to me, isn't it? You wanted my protection.'

'Yes, that's all true. I was honest about that right from the start. But I didn't want those things at the expense of a little girl's happiness. A little girl who has already suffered a major trauma in her life.' Layla was shaking so badly she wasn't sure her legs would hold her. 'There is no way I would have foisted myself on her as a stranger. At the very least I would have suggested I take time to get to know her. To gain her trust.'

'That would have created a delay we could not afford, and this was never about building a relationship. And you are assuming you would have gained her trust.'

'I would certainly have worked hard to do that. I have experience with children. Give me the opportunity and I will prove it to you.'

The shutters came down on those eyes. 'No. We will wait and see if the night terrors settle and then re-evaluate.'

'Perhaps they would settle if she had someone she could bond with. Someone she is close to.'

He turned slowly, his eyes like ice. 'My relationship with my daughter is very close.'

'Yes, I can see that.' She thought about the way he'd soothed the child. About the anxiety and love on his face and the patience he'd shown. It had warmed her because she'd never seen a man like that with a child. 'But you're away a great deal. You have your business interests—'

'That is an inevitable part of life. When I can, I take her with me, and when I can't I make sure I return here as quickly I can.'

'But when you are away who looks after her?'

He didn't answer immediately. 'She is with Nadia, who loves her very much.'

Nadia?

Layla felt as if she were walking on eggshells. This wasn't the time to point out that Nadia had seemed out of her depth at the moment of crisis. 'How have you kept Zahra's existence a secret?'

'I have the support of many people.'

'But I don't.'

He glanced at her with a frown. 'What does that mean?'

'No one speaks to me. This marriage has not been welcomed by the people who love you.' Suddenly she felt overwhelmed by it all. By the distance that couldn't be closed by physical intimacy alone. 'How can this possibly work even on the most basic level? If you don't trust me, why would they?'

'Because this union was never about trust.' He towered over her, powerful and imposing. 'Most of them understand why we did this. They know it is the right thing.'

But not all of them.

Layla thought about the hatred she sensed in Nadia and wondered again if the cause of it didn't go deeper than dismay at seeing the Sheikh marry the daughter of his enemy.

'So what happens now? You have a daughter. Are you saying you don't want me to meet her?'

'For the time being, no. She is already having night terrors. I don't want to risk making those worse by introducing you to her.'

His belief that she might make it worse hurt more than she would have thought possible, but how could she, of all people, blame a man for wanting to protect his child?

She'd never had that and she felt the loss of it keenly.

'Of course, if that is what you prefer.' Layla's jaw was stiff, her thoughts a mess of pain as she thought what she would have given to have a father who fought so fiercely to protect her from harm. 'But I don't think it's the right decision.'

'You think you know better than me what is right for my child?'

'No, what I think is that you don't know me at all. You married me with a set of preconceived ideas of who I am, and I don't blame you for that, but we're married now and for this to work you have to start seeing me. The real me. I may not be able to swim or ride a horse, but I am good with children. I think if we are to become a family we need to start somewhere.'

'We have started somewhere.'

His gaze shifted to the rumpled sheets and then back to her and she felt a tiny shiver run through her. Right now he was distant and intimidating but she knew it wasn't fear that made her knees weak. Looking into those brooding black eyes, gazing at the dangerous curve of his sensual mouth, all she could think of was how it felt to have those lips on her body, how it felt when he filled her, possessed her, drove her mindless. Her skin still burned from his touch. Her head was dizzy with the memory of how he made her feel and she slid her fingers into her hair and shook her head in frustration.

'A relationship cannot just be about sex.'

His eyes held hers, hard and unsympathetic. 'It has to be, because I can give you nothing else.'

In the morning he was gone again.

If she'd thought their shared confidences would have moved their relationship forward, she was disappointed.

And this time when she heard children laughing she knew one of the voices belonged to his daughter.

It felt unnatural not to approach her and build a relationship, but he'd made his wishes clear on that matter so Layla sat in the shade on a smooth rock by the oasis and forced herself not to initiate contact with the little girl. And she seemed happy enough, playing with her friends, laughing as a child should laugh. Laughing without fear that the sound might draw unwanted attention.

The child laughed until darkness fell over the desert.

And then the screams started again.

Instinct drove Layla from her bed. Heart pounding, she came to a screeching halt outside the entrance to the tent.

He didn't want her near his daughter, did he?

Unless she wanted to create a rift between them she had to respect that decision.

Torn, she stood there, waiting for the child's screams to settle, telling herself that Nadia was there and would comfort the girl.

The screams grew louder and more desperate.

Sweat beaded on Layla's forehead. Just listening to it stressed her so badly her heart raced. The sound reminded her so much of Yasmin in the early days, and to stand there and do nothing demanded a self-control and thick skin Layla didn't possess.

Pressing her palm to her forehead, she breathed deeply and tried to calm herself. She told herself it wasn't her concern, that if she suddenly appeared in the tent it would probably just frighten the child even more. But none of that reasoning did anything to ease her urge to do something.

Why didn't someone else go to her? *Where was Nadia?*

Her will-power stretched taut, she lasted another five seconds before giving in. If Raz never spoke to her again, so be it. He hardly spoke to her anyway so it wouldn't be that much of a loss.

As she pushed aside the flap she expected to see Nadia, but the tent was empty apart from the little girl who sat alone in the enormous bed, shuddering and screaming at some imaginary terror. At her feet lay the two Saluki, whimpering and looking at the child in alarm and confusion, as if they sensed a threat but couldn't identify it.

Mouth dry, Layla stared at the dogs. Nothing but a screaming child could have propelled her forward.

Her heart was kicking at her ribcage—not just because to get to the child meant stepping over fur and teeth, but because the sound of the screaming brought back so many memories of Yasmin, terrified and clinging to her.

She threw one last glance over her shoulder, in case there was someone else who could do this, but there was no sign of Nadia or the bodyguards who were supposed to be in attendance.

Trying to look confident, she stepped over the Saluki as gracefully as a ballerina, braced to feel those sharp teeth close around her ankle.

The dog closest to the bed growled, a menacing rumble low in its throat, but it didn't move from its position.

Taking that as a good sign, Layla crawled onto the bed and snuggled down with the child, stroking her back and talking to her, hoping desperately that the tone of her voice would do the trick and the child wouldn't wake and realize that the comfort came from a stranger.

'There, you're safe now—and you need to go back to sleep.' She talked nonsense, and then decided a story might help. 'Once upon a time...' She told the same stories she'd told her sister at the same age, remembered them word for word, and the familiarity of the ritual soothed her as well as the child. She talked quietly until the little girl's breathing suggested she was deeply asleep while all the time the two Saluki lay by the bed, heads on paws, watching her.

Afraid that if she moved she'd wake the child, Layla stayed still, her fingers tangled in the dark curls that belonged to Raz Al Zahki's daughter. Looking down at that sweet, vulnerable face, now smeared with tears, she felt her heart twist.

What had she been through?

What had she suffered?

She'd stay just a while. Until she was sure the girl was asleep.

Then she'd return to her bed and he wouldn't be any the wiser.

The red ball of the dawn sun was rising up behind the mountainous dunes when Raz rode back into the camp two days later. His eyes were gritty from lack of sleep, his head pounding following long days spent in meetings with senior tribal members.

He needed sleep, but nowhere near as much as he needed a swim.

It was still early and everything was quiet and still. No one was stirring.

Having handed over his stallion to one of the waiting grooms, he made straight towards the tent where his daughter slept, noticing with a frown that there was no sign of the guard.

Fear for his daughter fuelled his stride.

Entering quietly, he stood for a moment on the threshold, his eyes adjusting to the dim light, relieved to see the dogs sprawled protectively at the foot of the bed.

The familiar sight of the lump in the bed brought relief rushing down on him—and then he realised that the lump was bigger than usual.

Stepping closer, he saw that there in the bed, with her arms wrapped around his daughter, was Layla.

Shock and surprise were replaced by anger, and then another, darker emotion he didn't dare examine too closely.

The dogs sensed the change in his mood and growled, and those growls woke the child. Her expression brightened as she saw her father and she sat up sleepily, the movement waking Layla.

Her eyes opened and her gaze met his, blank at first and then alight with consternation.

Sitting up, she clutched at the sheet. 'We weren't expecting you so early.'

'Evidently.' His tone was silky soft and he saw the colour return to her cheeks as she met his hostile gaze.

'I'm *pleased* you're early.' Zahra slid out of the bed, paused to hug and kiss the dog closest to her, and ran across to him, arms outstretched. 'Has Shakira had her foal?'

'Not yet.' Raz scooped her into his arms. Her hair brushed against his jaw and he felt his insides knot with love. It was a love that overwhelmed every emotion he'd ever felt. A love that made a strong man vulnerable. And he felt that vulnerability now as he held her and felt those slender arms tighten around his neck.

'When can we go and see her?'

'Soon.' He hugged her protectively, his eyes still on the woman in the bed. 'Zahra, I want you to play with your toys for a minute while I speak to Layla.'

'Can't she stay?' Zahra was openly disappointed. 'She hasn't finished the end of the story. We both fell asleep.'

'I can finish it later.' Without meeting his eyes, Layla slid out of the bed.

He saw her hesitate before allowing her feet to touch the ground and saw her hold her breath as she stepped carefully over the dog blocking her path, as if doing so required nerves of steel.

Oblivious to the atmosphere, Zahra smiled at her. 'When you've finished talking, can we play in the sand like yesterday?'

The news that she'd been spending her days with his daughter was the final straw. 'No, you cannot, because we are going riding.'

'Together?'

'Together.' Touched by her expression of delight, he put her down gently. 'Play with Isis and Horus for a moment.'

She needed no encouragement to play with the dogs, and they in turn fussed around the child, proving themselves better guards than the people he'd paid to stand over her and keep watch in his absence.

Keeping his anger in check, he left the tent, noticing that

one of the guards assigned to watch over his daughter was now standing outside, having no doubt taken a badly timed bathroom break.

Deciding to deal with him later, Raz followed Layla to the edge of the oasis, noticing that she stopped a safe distance from the water's edge.

'You deliberately went against my orders.'

'Yes, I did.'

She turned to face him, her expression calm. She made no excuses. Nor did she apologise and that surprised him.

'I thought I'd made my wishes clear on this matter.'

'Would you rather I'd left your daughter to scream, Your Highness?'

The news that Zahra had been screaming again sent ice down the rigid length of his spine. 'If she was screaming then it would have been better for someone familiar to comfort her. That was your advice.'

'And I stand by it. But there was no one familiar. She was alone.'

'My daughter is never alone. She is under twenty-four-hour guard and Nadia is with her at all times.' Even as he said it he remembered that the guard had not been present when he'd arrived, and her next words confirmed that.

'She was alone last night. And the night before. And the night before that. There was no guard and there was no Nadia.' She seemed more annoyed than intimidated. 'You weren't here. I made the decision I thought was best, Your Highness.'

'My name is Raz,' he said tightly. 'I think we are now sufficiently well acquainted for you to use it.'

'Evidently not, since you don't see me as fit company for your daughter.'

Raz breathed deeply. 'Nadia is supposed to stay with her at night.'

'Then no doubt that is something you will wish to explore with her.'

Listening to that calm appraisal, Raz realised just how much he'd underestimated her. He'd mistaken silence for a lack of opinion, and shyness for a lack of forcefulness, but it seemed his new wife had a layer of steel, visible only if someone pressed hard enough. On this she wasn't budging.

'Nadia would not have left her alone.'

'Are you accusing me of lying?'

'Perhaps it was a simple misunderstanding. Perhaps she went to fetch Zahra a drink or something to eat.'

'There was no sign of her at any point during the night, nor of the guard. I understand that as her nanny you believe Nadia to be the best person to care for her, but I'm providing you with evidence that she left the child alone. Why would you doubt me?'

'Because Nadia isn't Zahra's nanny. She is her aunt.' That confession was met by a tense silence.

For a moment she said nothing and simply stared at him. Then her mouth moved and finally words emerged.

'Her *aunt*?'

Raz stayed perfectly still. 'Nadia is my late wife's sister.'

'S-sister?' She stammered the word, visibly shocked. Again she said nothing, and then she shook her head briefly. 'And you didn't think that was worth mentioning? You let me turn up here in my wedding dress and you didn't even *warn* her or tell me who she was?'

'When would I have had the opportunity to warn her? We were married only hours after you appeared unannounced at my desert camp. Then we arrived here and she came out of the tent before I had a chance to speak to her privately.'

'It is no wonder she can barely look at me.' Her words were barely audible. 'It explains so much.'

'It does *not* explain why she would leave Zahra unattended.'

'Maybe it does. Maybe...' She frowned slightly and then stared at the still surface of the oasis. 'You should have told me. There is *so much* you should have told me.'

'Why would I tell you?'

'You really have to ask me that?' Her head was turned towards him, pain and accusation in her eyes. 'Because keeping secrets is doing nothing but harm. I understand that this is hard for you, I understand that you have to make love to me in the dark because touching me makes you think of your wife and that makes you feel guilty, and I understand that you don't want to be here during the day because it's like a slap every time you look at me. I understand that, given the way you feel about my family, you are reluctant to trust me with your child. I don't blame you for that. But it wasn't Nadia who comforted Zahra in the night, Your Highness. It wasn't Nadia who read to her and played with her. For the past two days it hasn't been Nadia who has cared for your daughter. It has been me.'

Raz was stunned into silence by her interpretation of the facts, but before he could respond she took a step closer to him.

'Do you think I'm not a caring person? Is that what you think?' Her voice vibrated with tension. 'Do you think I would have crossed a desert I didn't know, on a horse I had no idea how to ride, to find a man who hates me, if I weren't a caring person? Just in case the facts don't speak for themselves, let me tell you I'm a *very* caring person—and if you looked at the facts you'd be able to see that. And, yes, I was thinking of my sister and my future, but I also care about the people of Tazkhan. And before you dismiss that, based only on my bloodline, let me remind you that we can choose many things in life, but whom we are related to isn't one of them. I chose to go to your daughter in the night because I couldn't sit there and listen to her distress. And I chose to step over those horrible, scary dogs in order to comfort her. So *never* imply I'm not trustworthy enough to care for you daughter.'

The stillness of the baking desert heat intensified the silence.

Raz stood still, her words stinging as they sank into his flesh. 'Why do you find the dogs scary?'

'After everything I just said to you, *that* is the question you choose to ask?' She gave a choked laugh—a sound loaded with disbelief—and he frowned.

'Layla—'

'No. Enough.' Her voice was shaky as she backed away from him. 'This conversation is going nowhere. You don't want to come anywhere near me and you can't bear it when I come anywhere near you, so just leave me alone.'

CHAPTER SEVEN

LAYLA PACED THE width of the tent and back again, so upset she didn't know how to calm herself. Once again she was ripped apart by emotions new to her and she tried desperately to rationalise them.

Why *would* he trust her? He didn't know her. Of *course* he'd be reluctant to allow her near his child—a child whose existence he'd taken great care to keep secret from her family. It was a sign of his love for his child, and she was the last person ever to criticise a father for loving his child.

So why did his attitude towards her hurt so badly?

And why couldn't she share the same space with him and not think about sex?

Hyped up and unsettled, she picked up a ripe peach from the bowl on the table and then put it down again, knowing that she was already in possession of the answer. And the answer was that it hurt so badly because it *felt* as if he cared. When his mouth was on hers, when his hands were holding her face and his body was buried deep in hers, it felt as if he cared. And it felt incredible. So incredible she wanted more. And in wanting more she also wanted it to mean something.

The whole thing was turning her brain into a churning mess. She was used to using logic, but the feelings inside her defied logic.

With a murmur of frustration Layla turned and paced back

again, trying to filter out the facts, but even the facts were confusing. To be so intimate in bed and so distant out of bed was muddling her brain. In bed, the signals were that he cared. Out of bed, it was clear he considered her on a level with the life forms occupying the bottom of the oasis.

Having admitted that to herself, it horrified her when he strode into the tent and closed the flap between them and the rest of the world.

'Go away—' Her voice cracked and she stepped back from him, still reeling from their conversation and feelings that were new to her. She wanted to turn them off and had no idea how. 'Don't say anything else. I can't take any more right now. I got the message. If you really don't want me near your daughter I won't go near her, but please make sure that *someone* does because I can't lie here listening to her screaming.'

'And that is very much to your credit.' His voice was low, his expression guarded as he watched her pace from one end of the tent to the other. 'I came to tell you that you're wrong.'

She couldn't focus.

She couldn't concentrate on the conversation because she wanted to look at him all the time. Not just because he was a man who naturally commanded attention, or even because he was sensationally good-looking—although that had to play a part—no, it was something so much more personal. It was because he knew her in a way no one had ever known her before. Whenever he was near she felt as if they were being pulled together. She had to fight the impulse to walk up to him and touch him. And because she had no experience of feeling that way she had no idea how to cure herself.

She'd never felt like this before and it was driving her mad. They had huge issues, but all she could think about was the feel of his hands on her and the way it felt to be kissed by him.

Layla pressed her fingers to her forehead, trying to clear her brain, trying to harness her old way of thinking. *Trying to push out thoughts she didn't want in her head.* Her stress levels were running into the red, her grip on control so loose she was afraid the whole thing was going to slip from her grasp. She knew the only way to pull herself back together was not to be near him. She needed to be on her own so that she could rebalance herself.

'I probably am wrong. You know Nadia much better than I do. I don't have all the facts. If you think she's the right person to care for your daughter, it's not my place to disagree with you.'

'I don't mean that you're wrong about Nadia. I mean that you're wrong about the other things you said.'

She was so aware of him standing there that the whole conversation blurred in her head. 'What things?' Was this the ultimate in humiliation? To know a man could do those things to her and feel nothing and yet still her head could be full of nothing but him? Why couldn't she detach the physical from the emotional as he evidently could?

The intimate atmosphere suffocated her, and the way he was looking at her made her feel as if he'd touched her skin with the flame of a candle.

'I make love to you in the dark *not* because I am thinking of my wife, but because you are very shy and I am trying to be sensitive to your feelings. On that first night you would not even remove your robe to show me your bruises, so I assumed you would want to take that side of our relationship very slowly.'

Slowly?

Layla felt as if she were burning up inside. She thought about what they'd shared. *Was that slowly?* Trembling, she hid her damp palms behind her back. 'Oh.'

'You came to me clutching a copy of the *Kama Sutra*, but you hadn't even glanced between the pages and clearly had no idea of what lay ahead of you. I decided you might be less self-conscious if you were in darkness.' He paused to draw breath. 'I don't spend time with you during the day, that is true, but it's because I have a million and one demands on my time—not least the upheaval in Tazkhan. I have spent the past two days meeting with certain members of the council in secret. Hassan has disappeared. That is another reason I am particularly concerned about my daughter's safety right now.'

Still dealing with the news that he'd been thinking of her feelings, Layla felt her stomach lurch. 'Hassan has disappeared?'

'Yes, and until we know his whereabouts I don't want my daughter left alone.' He hesitated. 'Or you. He is a desperate man. Who knows what he could decide to do, given that he now has so little to lose? He has lost any chance of taking your father's place and he has few, if any, supporters among the people. Speaking of which, I have been learning a great deal of interesting information about you in the past few days.'

'You have?'

'I spent some time with the people. I visited hospitals and local schools—including a school where you apparently help out.'

'I love books and I like to help the children who struggle with reading. The school doesn't have enough staff to offer that sort of help.' Layla stammered over the words, horrified that he'd found out with such ease. So much of her life had been conducted with discretion, if not secrecy. 'Who told you?'

'Apparently the staff don't feel the need to keep it a secret any longer as your father is dead and Hassan missing. There is no shortage of people willing to tell me how good you are with the children and what an excellent decision I made in marrying you.'

She stood rigid, thrown by that news. 'But *you* don't think that. I know you don't. On that first night you left the tent because you felt guilty about what we'd done.'

'No. I felt guilty because the sex was incredible. I agreed to this marriage because of what it meant for Tazkhan, but what we shared that night went well beyond duty and I couldn't pretend otherwise.'

Shocked into silence by his honesty, Layla tilted her head and stared up at him, feeling a shift in their relationship. 'I didn't know—'

'That I felt that way? I would have thought it was obvious.'

His dry tone made her blush and the look in his ebony eyes made her stomach flip.

'Your Highness—'

'Raz.'

He was standing so close to her she could hardly breathe. She lifted her hand and placed it on his chest, feeling the steady thud of his heart under her fingers. 'Raz.' It felt strange to say his name. Strange to be this close to someone.

He cupped her face in his hands. 'Do you realise that, despite the intimacies we have shared, that is the first time you have spoken my name?'

'It felt wrong to use your name. You were a stranger.'

There was a prolonged silence. His eyes dropped to her mouth. 'But I'm not a stranger now.'

His self-assurance was in direct contrast to her own mixed-up, tangled emotions.

'You hate me.'

'No. But I admit it's a complicated situation.' A wry smile tugged at his sensual mouth. 'You are a person who likes facts, so I will tell you that the facts in this case are that nothing is going the way I thought it would go when you turned up at my camp that night.'

She wanted to reach up and sink her hands into that glossy dark hair. She wanted to pull his head down to hers and see if his kiss felt as good in daylight as it did in darkness. She wanted to give herself up to the emotion and the confusion and stop trying to rationalise the mess in her head.

'It's not going the way I thought it would go, either.'

'I owe you an apology for ordering you to stay away from my daughter. You should know that I am very overprotective where she is concerned and the past week has been a particularly unsettling time.'

Standing this close to him, it was a struggle for her to concentrate. 'I would never criticise any father for being overprotective.'

'Please understand that my reluctance to allow you near her was less about you as an individual and more about my determination to keep life as stable as possible for her. I thought Nadia was the perfect person to care for her. It seems I may have been wrong.'

'Maybe you weren't. As you said, there is probably some perfectly reasonable explanation for her absence.' What right did she have to comment on the behaviour of another person when she didn't even understand her own?

'Possibly, but at the current time we are unlikely to find that out.' There was an edge to his tone. 'She has gone missing, along with one of my guards. I suspect that when they both should have been with Zahra they were together. We are trying to find them. In the meantime I must thank you for being so incredibly kind to my daughter when she was upset.'

His apology was as unexpected and unsettling as it was touching.

She'd craved distance, but instead she had closeness and a new sense of understanding that simply intensified the feelings inside her.

'She is very sweet and good-natured. And I love her sense of mischief. She reminds me so much of Yasmin.'

'The people here have noticed your kindness to her and it

has done much to make them warm towards you. What are these stories you've been telling Zahra that make her so desperate to go to bed at night?'

'*One Thousand and One Nights*. I read them to my sister.'

His eyes glittered. 'So now you think you are Scheherazade?'

'Hardly. But I thought if I could relax Zahra before she sleeps she might be less likely to wake.'

'It was a good plan. Did it work?'

'It's too soon to know. I just wish I'd brought the book with me instead of leaving it at the first camp.'

'That was the other book you brought with you?'

'Yes. It's one of my favourites. I decided I could only carry two, because of the weight, so I picked that one.'

His hands were still on her face, his gaze intent on hers. 'And the *Kama Sutra*.'

'It was a matter of priorities.' She knew her face was hot against his palm. 'And ignorance.'

'You have no need to explain yourself to me and no need to feel embarrassed.' His eyes darkened. 'These last few days have been a terrible strain for you. The threat of marriage to Hassan, whom you clearly fear and loathe, escaping from the palace, losing your sister in the desert and then being picked up by my men. Marriage to a stranger, a near drowning, and then living with a husband with whom you've barely shared a conversation but are expected to undress for.'

Layla tried to smile. 'When you put it like that, it's no wonder I'm a little wound up.'

'A little?'

'A lot. I'd be a lot better if there was news of Yasmin.'

His hand dropped from her face. 'So far there is none, but that does not mean you should worry. Salem is renowned for not communicating.'

Remembering the dark, forbidding profile of the man she'd

seen only briefly on that first night, Layla found that of little comfort. 'What if he can't find her?' She blurted the words out, seeking reassurance.

'If anyone can find her it will be Salem.' Raz hesitated, as if he were deciding how much to tell her. 'He has a special set of skills.'

'But what if Hassan has already tracked her down? What if he has her right now?'

'Then Salem will find *both* of them and you can safely feel sorry for Hassan.'

Layla hesitated, because to make an accusation unsupported by solid evidence felt wrong. 'I have nothing but instinct on which to base this suspicion, but I think Hassan may have played a part in the death of my father.'

His expression didn't change. 'I'm sure you're right.'

The relief that came from having someone to discuss it with was overwhelming. 'You suspect it too?'

'Of course. The moment I heard about the Sheikh's sudden illness it was the first thing that came to mind. We have no proof, but we believe it was Hassan who ordered someone to tamper with the brakes of my car two years ago. I don't believe it was his intention to kill or injure my wife, because that would have brought him no political benefit. There is little doubt I was the intended victim, but sadly she chose that day to borrow my car.'

His voice was thickened with a mix of regret, guilt and anger, his pain so powerful she felt it as if it were her own.

'I'm sorry.'

'I do not hold you in any way responsible. But it is true that Hassan would do anything for power. He and your father were cut from the same cloth.'

She knew that, but it was the first time she'd heard anyone else say it. 'If he finds my sister—'

'I would trust my brother with my life and we must now

trust him with your sister's life.' He turned to look at her, the lines of his handsome face set and serious. 'When did you last eat?'

'I'm not hungry.'

'You've barely eaten in the whole time we've been together.'

'I've eaten.'

'We may be in the dark for much of the time, but that does not make me blind.' His tone was dry. He hesitated. 'Zahra is keen for me to take her riding today. I know your experience with horses to date has been less than encouraging, but if you would like to learn to ride it would give me pleasure to teach you.'

The thought of spending yet more time on a horse horrified her, but she could tell he was reaching out to her and didn't want to do anything that could be considered a rebuff. 'Teaching a beginner would drive you mad.'

'I have been teaching Zahra since she was able to sit unsupported. Believe me when I say that nothing you throw at me can be more of a challenge than putting an overexcited toddler on a horse.'

'You taught her to ride that young?'

'It is the best age. She has grown up around horses, as I did. It wouldn't surprise me if she chooses to make that her career in some way in the future.'

Career?

'You see her having a career?'

'Of course. And I can't see it being diplomacy, because my daughter is as outspoken as your sister.'

That fact clearly amused him, and Layla thought about the times she'd had to haul Yasmin away from a situation before her comments created havoc.

'You're proud of your daughter.'

'Very.'

The contrast between his love for his daughter and her own barren childhood was so vividly accentuated that the breath caught in her throat. Wondering what was wrong with her that she could envy a child, Layla stepped away from him.

'Thank you for the offer of riding lessons, but I don't want to intrude on your time with Zahra.'

He curved an arm round her waist, trapping her. 'You're still upset?'

'No.' All she had around this man were uncomfortable feelings. Feelings about him. Feelings about herself. She'd arrived here thinking she knew herself well and had discovered she didn't know herself at all. It was like being inside the body of a stranger. 'I just don't want to intrude on your relationship with your daughter.'

'You were the one who pointed out that you should be part of my relationship with my daughter.'

Did it make her a bad person that it was almost too painful to watch? 'You have a very special bond.'

'A bond that will not be threatened or broken by the presence of another person.' His eyes narrowed. 'But that isn't the issue, is it? Tell me what's wrong.'

'There is no issue. Nothing is wrong.' She tried to walk away but he locked his arm tightly around her waist.

'Your father wanted you to marry Hassan, so I assume from that your relationship with him was difficult. You don't have to hide it from me. I want to know. All of it.'

'Why? What difference does it make?'

'As you just pointed out to me, keeping secrets isn't going to do anything for the progression of our relationship.'

Did he see a progression? This was a man who had loved his wife totally and completely. A man who had vowed never to love again. What progression could there be? She could have asked, but she wasn't sure she could cope with the answer. They were together now, and nothing could change that.

'My relationship with my father wasn't just difficult, it was non-existent. You're so proud of Zahra and you want the best for her.' She stared at a point in the middle of his chest, trying to contain her emotions and relate only the facts. 'My father was never proud of me. His interest in us extended no further than how useful we could be to him. He met Yasmin just four times in his life.'

Shock flared in his eyes. 'Four times? That is all?'

'Five, if you count the day he died, when we were both hiding behind the curtain in his rooms.' Layla was surprised by her sudden need to confide when she'd lived her life relying on no one.

There was a long, tense silence. 'I had no idea. I assumed—' He broke off and rubbed his fingers over his forehead, apparently struggling for words.

'I cared for Yasmin. We've never been apart. She's the only person in the world I've ever been close to until—' She stopped, feeling her face burn. *Feeling his eyes on her.*

'Until me.'

'I know we're not close in *that* sense,' she said quickly. 'I know what our relationship is.'

'Do you?' His voice was soft and his eyes didn't shift from her face. Slowly his hand dropped. 'Then you're making more progress than I, because I truly have no clue what our relationship is.'

The air was thickened with a tension she'd never felt before.

Something changed when she was with this man. Something she couldn't put a name too, and didn't understand.

She wanted desperately to reach out to him, to touch him as he'd touched her, but she wasn't sure he'd want that and didn't have the confidence to risk being rejected.

'You should go to Zahra.'

'You will come too. It would please her if you were to join us.'

'I really don't—'

'And it would please me, too. Get dressed and meet us outside. Zahra's favourite treat is to have breakfast by the oasis, so we will do that and then fly the helicopter to Bohara—my home.'

'You have a home?' It was something else she hadn't known about him. 'All the rumours are that you live in the desert and move around for your own safety.'

'I do live in the desert, and I do move around—because how else is a man expected to know his people if not by living among them? But I also have a place that is mine. A stud farm just inside the border with Zubran. On paper it is owned by the Sultan of that country, who just happens to be a friend of mine.' When Layla stared at him he flashed her a smile. 'I don't spend all my nights in a tent. After the last few days I think you deserve a taste of luxury.'

'Just practise everything I taught you. I will keep you on a leading rein so there is no way she can run away with you.'

'That's comforting to know.' Layla sat rigid on the calm, placid mare and Raz hid a smile, oddly touched by her determination to ride even though she clearly found the whole experience uncomfortable and unnatural. So far she had fallen three times, but each time she'd insisted on getting back on the horse.

'If you want to give up, just tell me.'

'I don't want to give up. I won't give up.' Her jaw was set, her wrists inflexible as she gripped the reins.

'Relax,' Raz said mildly. 'If you relax you will not fall.'

'We both know I am going to fall whatever I do.'

But still she got back up again. He wondered if that was a skill she'd developed during her loveless childhood. But it hadn't been completely loveless, had it? She'd had her sister. The sister who was now missing.

He made a mental note to try again to contact Salem, even though he knew such persistence would irritate his brother. 'Relax your wrists and lower your hands slightly.'

She did as he instructed. 'At least it isn't as far to fall as it is from your stallion.'

'I promise I will not let you fall again. Don't grip the reins so tightly—you're pulling on her mouth.'

'I am?' Dismayed, she immediately loosened the reins and rubbed the mare's neck by way of apology.

He watched, intrigued by her and wondering how such gentleness could come from so much evil.

In all the rumours that had oozed from the corrupt walls of the Citadel there had been little about the princesses and most hadn't thought to question the detail of their existence.

'You're doing well.'

'We both know I'm not doing well, but I will learn. Just as long as I don't hurt an innocent horse in the process.' She balanced herself carefully and then risked a glance at him. It was the first time she'd taken her eyes off the horse's ears. 'Thank you for being so patient.'

'You are very easy to teach because you listen. Sit up straight. Sit down in the saddle. That's good.'

Her jaw was rigid and he could see her concentrating, going through his instructions one by one. The mare walked forward without fuss, as accommodating as he'd known she would be.

'She's very pretty. Is she pure Arabian?'

'Yes. She is brave, spirited and intelligent, like all of her breed. And very strong. She could carry you for days in the desert and not tire. It's the reason we choose this breed for endurance racing.' It occurred to him that she shared many of those qualities. 'The Arab horse is surefooted and agile in difficult terrain and bred for stamina. It can withstand the daytime heat of the desert and the cold at night.'

'You bred her?'

'My father bred her. He gave her to me as a foal but I am too heavy for her now. She taught Zahra to ride.'

'You mean *you* taught her.'

'The horse did most of the teaching.'

'Did your wife ride?'

She asked the question quietly and he realised how sensitive the situation must be for her.

'She didn't ride, but she was an artist and she loved to paint the horses. She spent hours studying equine anatomy and her attention to detail was astonishing. Her mother was an artist, too, and she always hoped that Zahra would be equally artistic. But Zahra only ever wanted to ride the horse, not immortalise its image on paper.'

'The greatest gift a parent can give is to allow a child to be who they want to be.'

Her wistful tone caught his attention.

'You have told me about your father, but nothing about your mother.'

'My mother died just after I was born.'

'So your sister—?'

'Yasmin is my half sister. Her mother was a model who caught my father's attention for a short time. She left when Yasmin was five and we haven't seen her since.'

It was a brief delivery of the facts, devoid of emotion, but he could imagine how much emotion was simmering below the composure that seemed to be part of her. *She'd learned to hold it all in*, he thought. *Learned to feel without expressing the feeling.*

'But you said *you* cared for your sister. How is that possible?'

She sat without moving, her gaze focused on the horse's ears. 'It's possible.'

'You were seven and she was five.'

'We learned what we had to learn.'

The mare, perhaps sensing the sudden tension of her rider, threw up her head and he saw Layla's fingers whiten on the reins.

'She is the most reliable horse in my stables, but if you feel unsafe you can always grab a piece of her mane.'

'It doesn't seem fair to make her suffer just because I'm nervous.' But her fingers closed gently and carefully around a hunk of the mare's mane.

Watching her, Raz felt himself harden. His gaze focused on those slim fingers. Heat shot through him as he remembered how those fingers felt against his skin.

He lifted his gaze from her fingers to her face, studying the curve of her cheek and the sweep of her inky lashes, and she must have felt his scrutiny because she turned her head and her eyes met his.

Raz felt that look all the way through him.

'Can she gallop yet?' Zahra cantered up, disturbing the moment, glued to the back of her horse as if she'd been born in the saddle, Isis and Horus running by her side. 'I want you to learn fast, Layla, so we can ride together. Isis and Horus can come with us too. They love it when we gallop.'

Layla had switched her attention from the horse to the dogs and Raz frowned.

'The dogs make you nervous?'

'I'm worried they might upset the horse.'

Her response made perfect sense, but he sensed something more and wondered if she'd been bitten as a child. That would certainly explain the fear he saw in her eyes whenever his dogs were nearby.

'Did you keep Saluki as pets when you were young?'

'No.' Her lips were bloodless, her slim fingers clenched in the horse's mane. 'Not as pets.'

'Layla…' He rode closer to her, his knee brushing against hers. 'If the dogs are a problem you must tell me.'

'The dogs aren't a problem. Zahra adores them and they adore her. They also guard her, which can only be a good thing.'

Her response was neutral and composed but he glimpsed something in her eyes—a shadow of something so dark and bleak he wasn't sure he even wanted to explore it further. He wondered again what her life must have been like. What it would have taken to drive someone like her to cross the desert to seek out a stranger.

The more he knew her, the more he realised that such impulsive behaviour was completely out of character. She was a woman who thought everything through, who relied on evidence to make decisions, and yet she'd chosen to risk everything to find him. She'd known nothing about him, and yet she'd preferred to commit herself to the unknown than spend another day in her old life. *So what did that say about her life?*

'When can we gallop?' It was Zahra who asked the question, circling her pony like a polo player as she waited impatiently for her father.

'Later,' Raz told her. 'I don't want to leave Layla.'

'Don't worry about me. I think I might have had enough for one day and so has this poor horse.'

Apparently relieved to have an excuse to finish, she rode the mare to a halt the way he'd taught her.

'You two gallop and I'll go back. See you at the stables. But I think I'll walk and lead her, if that's all right.'

Before she could dismount, Raz reached out and covered her hand with his.

'You are doing well.'

Her mouth twitched at the corners. 'We both know I'm
doing terribly,' she said dryly, 'but thank you for saying that.'

'It's always harder to learn as an adult than as a child because your awareness of danger is more sharply focused.'
And he suspected her awareness of danger was even more
sharply focused than most. He watched her face, searching
for clues, but her expression didn't change and he released
her hand. 'Go and relax. Abdul will show you my library.'

'You have a library?' Her face brightened but Zahra shud-
dered.

'Who wants books when they can have horses?'

CHAPTER EIGHT

LAYLA SAT CURLED up on a low ottoman covered in rich red silk, a stack of books awaiting her attention and a chilled fruit juice on the table in front of her. Of all the rooms in Raz's beautiful home—*the home she hadn't known existed*—the library was predictably her favourite. Not just because of the walls lined with books, but because of the views. The doors opened over a courtyard with a central fountain that sent cooling water flowing over a majestic statue of a horse. And now, with the sun setting over the distant dunes, the courtyard was floodlit with a warm golden light.

It was the most beautiful place she'd ever seen.

On their arrival Raz had been called away, so it had been Zahra who had shown her round, predictably lingering in the stables and introducing Layla to every horse in the yard. The stables were beautiful, arranged around shady courtyards, and everywhere the sound of running water from fountains that offered a cool contrast to the parched desert.

After all the rumours about his Bedouin lifestyle she'd been surprised to discover that Raz owned a place like this, but what had really surprised her was the almost military efficiency with which it was run.

Here, horses were bred and trained in what was clearly a highly successful business. Smiling staff ran the place with smooth efficiency, allowing their elusive boss to come and go as security and his responsibilities demanded.

Used to the oppressive atmosphere of her rooms at the Citadel of Tazkhan, Layla felt a sense of peace and freedom she'd never experienced before. It wasn't just the ability to wander freely, but the absence of her father, Hassan, and all the others who had made her life so stressful.

She'd stood up, intending to explore the books on the higher shelves, when one of the dogs came bounding into the room, ears pricked.

Layla stood without moving and seconds later a woman rushed into the room and ushered the dog out, closing the door firmly behind the retreating animal.

'I apologise, Your Highness. I was feeding them and Horus went exploring. Please forgive me.'

Relieved that the overenthusiastic Horus was now on the other side of a closed door, Layla relaxed slightly. 'It's fine.'

'No, it isn't. His Highness left orders that the dogs weren't to be allowed near you. He was very strict about it. All the staff were informed.'

Layla stared at her. 'They were?' *He'd done that for her?*

'Yes, and I'm so sorry for what just happened.'

'Don't be.' She sank back down onto the sofa. She'd never given him an explanation for her fear of dogs, but he'd seen it and responded. She hadn't asked him to act, but he'd cared enough to instruct his staff to keep the dogs away from her. Realising that the girl was looking at her anxiously, Layla managed a smile. 'Don't worry. It's me, not the dogs. I'm sure the dogs are trustworthy.'

'Horus and Isis have had the run of this place since they were puppies, so it isn't always easy to keep them contained.'

'Keep who contained?'

Raz strode into the room at that moment wearing an exquisitely cut dark suit that suggested he'd come straight from meetings. His sudden appearance shattered her calm and sent her spinning straight back into that state of nervous tension that never seemed to leave her when he was around.

It was the first time she'd seen him since they'd arrived at his home but that didn't surprise her. She was fast coming to realise how hard he pushed himself and how seriously he took his responsibilities. Wherever he was, he rose before dawn, worked way past sunset, and still somehow managed to spend time with his daughter. Admittedly that time was usually spent galloping like two crazy people across the desert on horses that seemed half wild to her inexperienced eyes. His energy levels seemed limitless, his physical power, strength and stamina as much a part of him as those fierce black eyes that appeared to see under the surface she presented to the world.

And those eyes were on her now, stripping away her armour, seeing right through her. He saw her fear, knew how deeply that fear went, and the fact that he held that knowledge seemed as intimate as anything they'd shared in the darkness of the desert night. Somehow he'd accessed that most private part of her—her thoughts—and apart from her sister she wasn't used to sharing her thoughts with anyone. She wasn't used to revealing weakness. To do so made her feel as vulnerable as if she were standing naked in a crowd.

But he hadn't taken advantage, had he? He'd used the information, but he'd used it to her benefit not his. He hadn't mocked or ridiculed her response to the dogs. Instead he'd responded with gentleness and kindness. He hadn't just understood the depth of her fear, he'd tried to help.

The girl responsible for keeping the dogs under control was profuse in her apologies. 'I'm so sorry, Your Highness. Horus ran in here when my back was turned. I followed immediately,' she said quickly, 'and he didn't get farther than the door.'

Raz spoke in a low voice. Layla couldn't hear exactly what was said, but she saw the girl whiten and give a rapid shake of her head before backing away and leaving them alone.

'What did you say to her?'

He closed the door firmly. 'When I give an order I expect it to be obeyed, and I gave express instructions that the dogs were *not* to be allowed in the library or into whichever space you choose to occupy.'

'It's fine, really.'

His eyes held hers. 'But it isn't fine, is it? We both know it isn't fine even though you don't talk about it.'

Layla tried to steady her breathing but she knew it was a hopeless quest.

The moment it was just the two of them the atmosphere shifted.

She knew what sexual attraction was now. She knew it and she felt it right through her, from the tips of her fingers to the depths of her soul. It was the quickening of her heart when he walked into a room, the power of a shared look full of intimate promise. But most of all it was the constant long-ing to touch—the need to put her hands on his hard body and feel his hands on her. The craving was so intense it was al-most visceral, and it surprised her because she wouldn't have thought the physical could have so much power over her. The feelings thrilled her and scared her because they were unfa-miliar and uncontrollable.

Ignoring his reference to the dogs, Layla struggled to re-spond as her old self. 'Did you have a productive afternoon?'

'Yes, but the downside was that I neglected you on your first day here.'

'Zahra showed me round. We had fun together. And you don't have to worry about me—I'm used to occupying my-self.'

'In the past, yes, but I don't want your future to be like your past.'

She put down the book she was holding. 'I love books. I'm always happy to read.'

'Because it's an escape? Do you feel the need to escape when you're with me?'

'No.' Her mouth was dry. She had no way of telling him how much her feelings unsettled her because she could barely articulate it to herself. 'I don't only read to escape. I read be-cause I love the rhythm and flow of words. A good writer can create images with prose in the way an artist does with a brush.' And it was a good job she was a reader, not a writer, because she couldn't have found the words to describe how being with him made her feel.

'Then hopefully you can pass on some of your love of books to Zahra,' he said dryly, removing his tie and undoing his top button. 'To her, reading is an activity that takes her away from horses, which makes it something to be loathed and detested.'

'So we need to start by finding her some horse fiction.'

'Horse fiction?' His brows rose. 'Does such a thing exist?'

'Of course.' It was a relief to have something to focus on. She dragged her eyes from the addictive curve of his mouth and tried not to think how it felt when he kissed her. 'There are talking horses in *The Horse and His Boy* by C.S. Lewis, and I always loved *Black Beauty* because the story is told from the horse's point of view. I'm sure I can think of more.'

His eyes gleamed dark, his gaze disturbingly compelling. 'In that case you are now officially responsible for Zahra's reading—or lack of it.'

'It will be my pleasure. It's just a question of finding some-thing to engage her interest. She is enjoying the stories I'm telling her at bedtime.'

'And on that topic...' He strolled across the room to her

and handed her a package. She unwrapped it cautiously, wondering how she hadn't noticed that he was holding something in his hand.

'Oh!' As the packaging fell away she felt her breath catch. 'It's my copy of *A Thousand and One Nights*. I thought it was lost forever.'

'It came with us when we travelled on that first night. I should have given it to you before now but I didn't think of it.' He was standing close to her. So close it would have taken nothing to reach out and touch him. 'I'm sorry I've neglected you today.'

'You didn't neglect me. I understand the pressures on your time.' What would happen if she touched him? She had no idea of the etiquette and no idea how to subdue the feelings that threatened to overwhelm her. 'I hope your meetings went well.'

'Very well. What did you do this afternoon?'

'I read. Explored a bit. Enjoyed the surroundings. I've never been this close to the border with Zubran before. It's beautiful. You've known the Sultan and his wife for a long time?'

'Mal and I have been friends since childhood. I often stayed in his house. His father and mine were close—' He broke off but she read his mind easily.

'United against a common enemy,' she said quietly. '*My* father.'

'We are not going to talk about that now.'

He cupped her face in his hands and the touch of those strong fingers on her skin made her go hot inside.

Was that really all it took? One touch. One touch and she was hopelessly lost. Suddenly all she wanted was more. Just how badly she wanted more was embarrassing to contemplate.

'I moved Zahra into the room next to ours so that if she wakes we will hear,' she said.

His finger traced her jaw. 'That was thoughtful of you.'

'And I met your cousin,' Layla said desperately. 'The one who manages this place. She is very impressive. And she was welcoming. I didn't know you had business interests. Hassan has no idea you own this. No one does. No one knows you have a home here.'

'Have you finished?'

'Finished?'

Those dangerous dark eyes burned into hers. 'You are chattering and I've never known you chatter before. You're nervous.'

'I'm not nervous.'

'You can be honest with me. I *want* you to be honest.'

How honest? Was he waiting for her to admit she thought about him every moment of every day? Did he want her to say she just wanted to tear off his suit, his tie, his perfect white shirt and everything else he was wearing until the only thing between them was bare skin? What would he say if she confessed that night had become her favourite time? That she wished away every hour of daylight in the hope he might come to her?

'I'm not nervous.'

He stared down at her—held her eyes with his as if he were drawing all her thoughts inside him so that he could read them and know every detail.

Terrified of what he'd find inside her head, Layla tried to pull away. But his free hand slid behind her back and he locked her against him with a strong arm.

She felt the hardness of his powerful body against hers and goosebumps raced down her spine.

'Raz—'

'My daughter is asleep,' he said softly. 'We should probably move this conversation to the bedroom so that we can hear her if she wakes.'

The bedroom.

'Yes.'

Except that it felt so good being this close to him she didn't want to move. Didn't want him to let her go.

Fortunately when he did it was only briefly, and then he took her hand and drew her close to him as he led her from library to bedroom. She was aware of every movement he made. Aware that he shortened his stride to match hers, aware of the brush of his arm against hers as he stepped back to allow her through the door first, aware that he drew her closer as they passed the door of Zahra's bedroom and the sleeping forms of the ever devoted Isis and Horus.

'They are very protective of her.' She followed him into his luxurious bedroom and he closed the door behind them.

'It has been that way since she was a baby. I believe they would give their lives for her, but I am conscious that you are uncomfortable around them so I have given orders that they should not be allowed to roam freely.'

'Zahra's safety is more important than the fact I'm a little nervous with dogs. They must be allowed to do as they have always done.'

'A *little* nervous?'

His eyes were gently mocking and she gave a half smile.

'Terrified—there, I admit to being that pathetic.'

'*Not* pathetic. Nothing about you is pathetic.' His expression serious, he pulled her towards him. Tension shimmered between them. 'You accused me of turning out the lights so that I didn't know I was with you, but the lights are still on and if you want them turned off you're going to have to say so.' His eyes were dark on hers and the hunger she saw in him shocked and thrilled her.

'I don't want you to turn them off.' She wanted to see him. *All of him.*

'You're sure?'

'Yes.' Just as she was sure if he didn't kiss her soon she'd be the one to do the kissing. In fact she was close to doing just that when he cupped her face and lowered his head to hers.

His mouth was hot on hers, his kiss sure and clever, and just like every other time the explosion of sensation was instantaneous and all-consuming. Just like every other time her mind blanked. She felt dizzy with it, and the fact that this time there was no doubt he knew who he was kissing somehow intensified all those feelings.

As his mouth seduced hers she felt his palms on her shoulders, easing off the simple, modest dress she'd selected earlier that day, felt the skilled glide of his fingers down her spine. And this time, whatever happened to her, *whatever she felt*, she was determined not to close her eyes.

Perhaps he sensed it because he took her hand and placed it on his chest. 'Undress me.'

His soft command made her pulse sprint.

She felt the steady thud of his heart under her palm and then her shaking, useless fingers fumbled with first one button and then another. But the speed of her fingers wouldn't match the desperation building in her and she gave a murmur of frustration and tugged at his shirt, sending buttons flying.

Layla froze. 'I'm sorry.'

'For what?' His eyes glittered down at her. 'For wanting me as badly as I want you? That isn't something to apologise for.'

Releasing her briefly, he wrenched off his torn shirt, leaving her face to face with his muscular male chest. She stared at the dark hair that shadowed the centre of his chest and then narrowed down and disappeared below the waistband of his trousers.

She wondered if he was going to make the next move. Felt his eyes on her as he waited.

Face hot, Layla reached for the fastening of his trousers.

She heard the sharp intake of his breath, felt his board-flat abdomen tense against her fingers, and paused.

'Do it.' His tone was raw. 'Do what you want to do.'

She was too self-conscious to do *exactly* what she wanted to do, but she undid the button and slid down the zip, freeing him. The only sound in the room was the harsh rasp of his breathing and she heard the sound change as she took him in her hand and stroked him.

He felt hot and hard, and the thickness of him in her palm made her own body heat. It was the first time she'd touched him like this and for a moment she stood still, unsure of herself, and then he covered her hand with his and showed her, guiding her movements, teaching her what no man had taught her before. And she learned fast what pleased him, discovered the instant high that came from hearing the sudden intake of his breath or feeling the bite of his fingers in her flesh as he struggled for control.

Her palm cradling the most intimate part of him, she lifted her face to his. 'I'm sorry you have to teach me.'

'That proves how little you know about men, because I'm *not* sorry.' His tone was rough and his features were as tense as his shoulders. 'I am traditional enough to be pleased that everything my wife has learned in bed she learned from me.'

Layla hid a smile. 'That's not very progressive, Your Highness.'

'In some areas progress is overrated.'

'It's your own fault. If you'd let me keep the book—'

'You will not need a book.'

His tone thickened, he pulled her into him, taking her mouth in a hard, burning kiss before he tumbled her back onto the bed. Dispensing with the rest of his clothes, he came down on top of her, his weight pressing her into the soft mattress.

'Tell me if I'm too heavy for you.'

'You're not. I like it. I like the feel of you. All of you.'

His gaze darkened and he shifted slightly so that she felt the roughness of his thigh against the smoothness of hers. 'I promised myself I'd be patient.'

'You don't have to be patient.' Layla gazed into his handsome face, so hungry for him she ached in every part of her body. She slid her palm over the smooth skin of his powerful shoulder and felt the tension there, felt his own struggle to hold back. 'I don't need you to be patient.'

'If anything I do makes you uncomfortable—'

'It won't.'

She was about to say that nothing he did could make her uncomfortable but he was kissing her again, the slide of his tongue against hers driving all rational thought from her head. He kissed her with slow, deliberate expertise, and although he'd kissed her like this before she discovered that the light changed everything because now she could see. She kept her eyes open and so did he, and she could see the fire in his eyes, the flare of heat as he looked at her, the raw hunger that she knew was mirrored in her own gaze.

She needed to see him.

Needed him to see her.

And if she'd been worried he couldn't look at her she wasn't any more, because it was soon obvious he couldn't *not* look at her as he slid down her body, exploring every shivering, trembling inch while the lamps threw golden shadows over her skin.

Layla watched as his fingertips grazed her nipples and then felt the skilled flick of his tongue. And then he took her in his mouth and the delicious heat of it intensified the ache in her pelvis until she was only able to stay still because the weight of his body was holding her down.

Her only outlet was to moan, and moan she did as she felt the brush of his erection against the soft flesh of her inner thigh. He eased away from her and slid his hand down one bare leg, parting her.

It was possibly the most intimate action of their relationship so far.

It was the first time he'd seen her. The first time any man had seen her. And she realised that the light offered no opportunity for modesty or concealment. Spread and exposed, there was no hiding, and when his gaze lifted to hers she knew her cheeks were burning.

'It makes me feel—'

'I know how it makes you feel,' he said softly, 'but you can trust me. I want you to trust me.'

Light shone from the two lamps positioned right by the bed. His eyes shifted from her flushed face to her breasts and lower still. To that part of her that lay between the shadows of her thighs—that part of her that now lay open to him. And if she were embarrassed it soon became clear that he wasn't. Nor did he intend to allow her to hide. Trembling with anticipation, she felt the warmth of his palm on the inside of her thigh, the gentle slide of skilled male fingers against her wet, sensitive flesh, and then he moved again and the next thing she felt was the scorching heat of his clever, knowing mouth.

Layla closed her eyes. He'd done this before but she was discovering that in the dark it was different. She knew how wet she was already, and then she felt his tongue on her and in her, parting her, exploring her in the most intimate way possible, until she was writhing against the silk sheets, only his firm grip on her hips keeping her still.

He drove her to orgasm again and again, and when he finally hauled her under him and thrust deep Layla was so dazed and disorientated, so weakened by pleasure, she could do nothing but move with him, lost in this new version of reality.

* * *

'Tell me about the dogs.'

He'd picked his moment carefully. Picked a time when she was at her most vulnerable. A time when she was more likely to trust him with those secrets she'd buried inside herself. Because she was wrapped in the curve of his arm he felt the tension ripple through her slender body as she tried to roll away from him.

'I can't.' The fear in her voice was so sharp it was almost visible.

'Try.'

'You don't understand—'

'I want to.' He wondered how far he could push before she shut herself down and refused him access. 'Were you bitten?'

Without warning, she pulled away from him and sat up. She stared blankly ahead of her and then drew up her knees and hugged them with her arms, as if giving herself comfort. 'When we were young Hassan used to make us play a game called Hide.'

'Hide and Seek?'

'*His* version of Hide and Seek. We were given an hour to hide and then—' The words seemed to jam in her mouth so he prompted her.

'Then they tried to find you?'

'Then they sent the dogs to find us.' Her voice was flat, the words factual, as if it were only by stripping out the emotion that she could bear to speak them. 'Saluki. Four of them. Although people keep them as pets, the Saluki is a hunting dog. But I'm sure you already know that. The Bedouin use them for hunting hares, gazelle, and foxes and other prey. In this case we were the prey.'

Shock stunned him into silence. When he finally managed to speak, he found himself devoid of words, because there simply were none. What could anyone say in response to a revelation of that magnitude? 'Layla—*habibti*—' The endearment flowed off his tongue so naturally he didn't notice. All his attention was focused on her.

'A Saluki is the fastest dog there is—did you know that?' She swept her hair away from her face with a shaking hand, her face ghostly pale in the dim light of the room. 'Some claim it's the Greyhound, but over long distances the Saluki is faster. Its paws are padded so they absorb the impact. Believe me when I say that no child, however terrified, could ever outrun a Saluki. I know because we tried.'

She was speaking quickly now, her breathing shallow, as if she were remembering what it was like to run with fear in her heart and menace at her heels.

The image she painted was so vivid Raz felt nausea settle in the pit of his stomach. He sat up slowly, staring at her frozen profile. 'You are saying he sent the dogs to hunt you?'

'It was Hassan's idea of entertainment. Yasmin was terrified—just terrified.' Her teeth were chattering as she remembered. 'Her little body used to shake so badly she couldn't run, but it didn't really matter because running was pointless. And they didn't want us to run. They wanted us to hide. Do you know how terrifying it is, waiting for the moment when they find you? Because they *will* find you. And you hear them before you see them—you hear them panting, and the muffled thud of their paws as they pick up the scent and follow your trail. And you brace yourself for that moment, never knowing if this time they'll rip you apart before the humans call them off. All you can do is close your eyes and hope.'

For the first time he noticed a mark on her upper arm—an old scar, a silvery twist of damaged flesh that ran from shoulder to elbow. Lifting his hand, he touched it with his fingertips and felt her flinch. 'They did this?'

'I used to lie on top of her...' Her voice whispered over the pain. 'And the dogs used to try and pull me off. And she was screaming and screaming and it drove the animals crazy and I kept telling her not to move, to try and keep still, because it made it worse. But it was impossible to lie still when you could feel the heat of their breath on your neck and hear that horrible, rumbling growl—'

It explained her behaviour whenever Isis and Horus were around. She was always still. She never moved. It explained her behaviour on that first night in the tent when she'd been frozen to the spot and he hadn't understood why.

Now he understood, and his anger was black and lethal as he pulled her into the circle of his arms, holding her as she shivered and shook. 'I will find him,' he vowed in a thickened voice. 'I swear to you I will find him and he will pay for what he did to you both.'

'He is already paying. What he wanted was power and he's lost that. Between us we've taken that from him and it feels good.'

'I will not allow Isis and Horus near you again.'

'I don't want that. I want to get used to them.' Her voice was fiercely determined. 'I *need* to get used to them. They're good dogs. I know they are. Nothing like the others.'

Her lips were bloodless, her eyes dark and bruised in the soft light. She was so pale he felt guilt rip through him

'I shouldn't have made you talk about it, *habibti.*'

'You were right to make me talk about it. Why should I expect you to share things with me if I share nothing with you? On that first night you asked why a woman would cross a desert on a horse she couldn't ride to find a man she didn't know. Now you know the answer.'

'Your father knew what Hassan did?'

'My father had no interest in us beyond our use to him in his political games.'

'I am starting to understand the reason for your sister's night terrors.'

'That was just part of it.' She eased away from him, her eyes wide with anxiety. 'You don't think Salem would use dogs to track her?'

'No. You can rest assured that Salem utilises far more sophisticated methods than dogs. By now he will have tapped his many contacts in various shadowy government organisations and be using the most up-to-date technology that exists.'

'I let her down. I was the one who made the decision to leave the palace, and because of me she is lost and alone.'

'You made the right decision. By leaving you took control away from Hassan.' He smoothed her hair with his fingers and lay down in the bed again, taking her with him. Keeping his arm round her, he pulled the covers over them. 'You're safe. I'll never let him touch you again. This is your life now. This is your home.'

'But when everything settles in Tazkhan you will have to move there. The people will expect it.'

Her voice was muffled against his chest and Raz stared up at the ceiling, the scent of her hair winding itself around his senses.

'It's what we do that matters, not where we live. We will sort something out that works for everyone. And in the meantime I'm going to make you forget that life. This is your life now and, yes, there is responsibility—but there should also be fun.'

'Fun?'

She sounded unsure, doubtful, as if she had no idea what he meant, and he realised how little thought he'd given to her life and just how wrong he'd been in the few thoughts he'd had.

'Dancing? Talking to new people? Wearing nice clothes?'

'I've never danced. I'm not sure I'd be very good at it if my experiences on a horse are anything to go by.'

'You've never danced?' His arms tightened around her. 'Then that's something else I need to teach you. Now, go to sleep. You're safe now, I promise.'

CHAPTER NINE

SHE WOKE ALONE and the level of disappointment that followed that discovery was shocking. And then she heard the
sound of the shower and realised he was using the bathroom.

He hadn't left.

For once he hadn't walked away once the sun had risen.

Layla rolled onto her back and stared up at the ceiling,
her head full of the night before. And not just because of the
discovery that she had an unsettling capacity to enjoy sex.

He'd called her *habibti*.

It was the first time he'd called her that. She subdued the
sudden lift of her mood with cold, calm logic. She'd been
upset. Whatever lay between them, Raz Al Zahki was a decent human being. The endearment had been spoken out of
comfort, not affection, and she'd be deluded if she pretended
otherwise.

But it had been the first time in her life anyone had held
her like that. The first time anyone had offered comfort.

And it had felt good.

And strange. She'd never shared her thoughts with another
person. Not even Yasmin. Because her role had been to protect her sister, so she hadn't wanted to frighten her by revealing her own fears. Part of her felt vulnerable that she'd shown
him so much of herself, that he knew so much about her.

'Layla?' Zahra hovered in the doorway, clutching a book, unsure of her welcome.

When Layla sat up and stretched out her arms the little girl bounded into the room, closely followed by the ever-protective Isis and Horus.

Despite her best efforts Layla felt her throat close and the fear spark inside her.

'*Bas!* Stop!' Raz thundered the command from the door-way of the bathroom and the dogs skidded to a halt, crashing into each other like clowns in a circus. There was something almost comical about the dopey way they looked at him but he didn't smile. 'Sit and stay, or tonight you'll be sleeping in the desert.'

The dogs gave a whine and obediently sank down, heads on paws.

Layla felt her heart-rate slowly normalise.

Raz transferred his gaze to her and she knew he was think-ing about her confession of the night before, so she smiled and tried to keep it light. 'They know who's boss.'

'My dad is the boss. Everyone does as he says except me.' Zahra climbed onto the bed, still holding her book. 'Can we finish the story you started last night? You stopped at the exciting bit.'

Layla shifted across in the bed, relieved she'd thought to put her nightdress on in case Zahra woke in the night.

She was desperately conscious of Raz watching her, his bare chest still damp from the shower, a towel knotted around his waist.

'You can read for a while but then you need to pack.'

'Pack?' Zahra lost interest in the book. 'We're going on a trip? Can we ride?'

'Not this time. We're flying to Zubran for a party tonight.'

Zahra's face fell. 'A party? That means I can't come.'

Raz strolled across the room and scooped his daughter into

his arms. 'You can't come to the party but you can come to Zubran. I need you there. I want your opinion on a mare I'm thinking of buying.'

Watching the two of them together, Layla felt something soften inside her. The fact that a father could care so much about his daughter's feelings and opinion was a revelation. It was something she hadn't witnessed before because she'd had no relationship with her own father.

Aware that Raz was looking at her with question in his eyes, she smiled. 'You are buying another horse? How many animals can one person ride?'

'She won't be for riding. She'll be for breeding,' Zahra told her seriously. 'I'm going to have a foal of my own to take care of. I'm going to pack right now.' Squirming out of her father's arms, she sped from the room.

Overwhelmed by emotions so intense and uncomfortable she could hardly handle them, Layla rescued the book from where it lay as the little girl had left it, in danger of snapping its spine.

'Layla?' His voice was soft. 'Talk to me.'

What was there to say? 'You're a good father.' The words were thickened by the lump in her throat. 'And she adores you.'

'You think that's a bad thing?'

'Oh, no! How could I? A little girl *should* adore her daddy.'

There was a tense silence. 'But it doesn't always happen that way, does it?'

'No. But life is full of things that shouldn't happen—as we both know.' She closed the book carefully. 'If you want me to encourage her to read, it's probably best not to mention the word *horse* while we have a book open.'

'I know, but in this case it was intentional.' The corners of his mouth flickered. 'I wanted her out of the room. I need to talk to you, *habibti.*'

Habibti.

Her stomach flipped. What reason did he have to call her that this morning? Or did he think she still needed the comfort? 'What about?'

'I want to make sure you are comfortable about tonight.'

'The party? What exactly does it involve?'

'It is a fundraiser for a children's charity supported by the Sultan of Zubran and his wife, Avery. I think you'll like her. She used to run a highly successful party planning business and her events are always spectacular. This one promises to be no exception.'

'A fundraiser?' Layla felt no excitement. Just pressure. 'What exactly is my role at an event like that?'

'Your role is to enjoy yourself. Something I suspect you haven't done anywhere near enough in your life.' Droplets of water clung to his powerful shoulders and his hair was still sleek and damp from the shower. 'Did you never attend formal functions at the Citadel?'

'Never. My father never raised funds for anyone except himself and neither did Hassan.' Thinking of Hassan made her feel sick, and this time her concern wasn't just for herself and her sister. 'If you appear in public at a high-profile event like this one, won't you be a target?'

'The only people who know in advance that we will be there are the Sultan himself and his wife. I would trust them with my life. *Have* trusted them with my life on more occasions than I care to count. And although I take sensible precautions I don't live my life in hiding. I am easy enough to find if someone knows where to look.'

As they both knew.

Their eyes met briefly and she felt a new intimacy—and something she hadn't felt before. A warmth. *A new level of understanding.*

And something else. A chemistry so intense it thickened

the air and created a tension that unsettled her. They were talking about serious issues and yet part of her just wanted to place her hand on the hard swell of his biceps and her lips on the dark haze of hair at the centre of his chest.

'What about Zahra?' Somehow she managed to speak. 'What will she do while we're at the party.'

'She will be safe in Zubran. She has been there many times and it is sufficiently familiar that hopefully her night terrors will not return.' His gaze lingered on her face. 'Since you started reading to her at night and settling her down there have been no more bad dreams.'

'I know. And I'm pleased.'

'I can't thank you enough.'

'No thanks are needed.'

'And now it is your turn,' he said softly. 'We need to replace those bad dreams of yours, and those memories, with something much happier. Starting with this party.'

'But if Hassan guesses where you are going—'

'I don't anticipate that Hassan will pay us a visit, but if he does then it will save us the bother of finding him.' His gaze held hers for a moment. 'So, how do you feel about the party? I don't want to overwhelm you, and I know how anxious you are for news of your sister, but I would very much like you to have fun and enjoy yourself.'

Layla couldn't imagine enjoying herself in the company of a large number of strangers but she didn't want to say so. 'I'm already looking forward to it.'

'I've promised to take Zahra riding this morning. Will you join us?'

Was it her imagination or had those dark shadows she saw in his eyes lessened? Was it wishful thinking on her part to think he seemed happier and more relaxed?

'I think the two of you should ride together.'

'Join us.' He brushed her cheek with the backs of his fingers. 'Abdul will stay with you and we will all ride slowly.'

But of course he didn't know the meaning of *slow*, pushing his animal to the limit as he sped into the distance in pursuit of his young daughter, who seemed to embrace their extreme ride with the same enthusiasm as her father. The horse's tail was lifted high and trailed like a banner in the wind, his curved neck betraying his enviable lineage. Even Layla, whose knowledge of horses came entirely from books, could see the animal was beautiful.

It made her sick with nerves just watching, but she had to admit it was good that Zahra didn't seem afraid either of horses or the Saluki who ran next to them.

If her childhood had been different would she have been the same?

Would she be the one galloping across the sand and whooping with excitement?

'You are doing so well, Your Highness.' It was Abdul, as kind and solicitous as ever as he rode by her side as Raz had instructed.

'We both know I'm not, but thank you for the encouragement.' She stared enviously at Raz and Zahra, now just specks in the distance.

'We are all born with different gifts,' Abdul said quietly. 'His Highness has a particular gift with horses, but he has also had the benefit of many years of experience. He was virtually raised on horseback. The moment he could sit unsupported he was put on a horse—I think he was about six months old. He rode with his father every day until he could control the animal himself. Then he rode alone. And he has a tendency to take what many would see as appalling risks, so I would beg you do *not* aspire to emulate him.'

'Not much chance of that.' She felt a pang that she wasn't confident enough to share that interest with him, but she knew that even if she rode each day and every day for the rest of her life she'd never be as good as Raz.

'You have your own gifts.' Abdul reached across and showed her how to shorten the reins. 'And those are to be valued every bit as much as His Highness's skills with a horse. You have courage and patience, as you have shown on numerous occasions over the past week. His Highness is growing more relaxed by the day and we have you to thank for that.'

'You think so?' Perhaps it hadn't been her imagination. 'Will you be coming with us to Zubran?'

'Yes, because His Highness will have talks with the Sultan.'

'And will you be at the party, Abdul?'

'Sadly, no, Your Highness. But I feel sure you will enjoy it.'

'Will I?' Layla wasn't convinced. 'I have no idea what I'm supposed to wear.'

'On that topic I have taken the liberty of contacting Her Royal Highness the Sultana of Zubran. She has generously agreed to assist with your wardrobe needs as there has been no opportunity to provide what you will require for such an event.'

'I don't want to put her to any trouble.'

Abdul cleared his throat. 'Perhaps it is indiscreet of me to say this, but I can assure you that there is nothing Her Highness enjoys more than dressing people in clothes of her choosing. Zahra loves going to see her for that very reason. And you will find Her Highness to be a very warm and caring person once she has finished organising your life and telling you what you should be doing.'

Layla was amused and intrigued. 'So she isn't dominated by the Sultan?'

'It is very much a marriage of equals,' Abdul said dryly, and Layla felt her heart squeeze as she watched Raz ride into the distance.

Theirs wasn't a marriage of equals, was it?

She couldn't ride. She couldn't swim. She was terrified of his dogs. She had no idea what was expected of her at this party.

What exactly *did* she have to offer him?

The realisation that she was hopeless at all the things that were important to him disturbed her, as did the thought that tonight they would be making their first public appearance together.

Never having been allowed to mingle with her father's guests, Layla felt as if she were back in the oasis with the waters closing over her head.

'I'd be delighted if Her Highness would help me with my wardrobe.'

If it came to a choice between inconveniencing the Sultan's wife and embarrassing Raz she'd pick inconvenience every time. But as it turned out Abdul was correct in his summation that their hostess would be only too delighted to take responsibility for her wardrobe.

'You've been hiding out in the desert together? I have never heard anything more romantic in my life! But romance can only take a girl so far and then she needs a decent spa day.'

Avery was the most elegant, capable, efficient person Layla had ever met, and within minutes they were curled up on a low sofa in an opulent room hung with beautiful tapestries and sipping tea.

'Mmm. Whenever we're in the desert Mal makes me drink the Bedouin variety, which is delicious, but you can't beat Earl Grey. Now, tell me all the details and leave nothing out.'

'Details?' Layla sat stiff and formal on the edge of the sofa, but Avery slipped off her shoes and curled her legs under her.

'I'm going to give you a tip, because once you and Raz are back in your rightful place in the palace at Tazkhan you're going to be throwing open those gilded doors and entertaining the whole world and your legs will feel as if they've been trapped between clamps: whenever you can before a big event take the weight off your feet. And now tell me if it's true that you escaped from the palace and rode into the desert on your father's wild stallion? It's too romantic for words.'

'It wasn't romantic. It was horrible in every way. And I don't think the horse was wild, precisely—at least not until we climbed on its back. Then it was certainly less than impressed—'

After a moment's hesitation Layla told Avery the whole story, and by the end of it she felt so relaxed she'd even removed her shoes.

'So you married for the good of Tazkhan, but now you're in love? That is the happiest ending I've heard in a long time.'

'Oh, no, that isn't true!' Startled, Layla stiffened. 'I'm not in love.'

Avery's brows rose. 'No? So when you say "Raz this" and "Raz that" in every sentence it's just because you're—' she waved a hand in the air '—sorry, but I only know one reason to mention a guy in every single breath and that's l-o-v-e. Either that or obsession, and you don't strike me as the obsessive type.'

Love? Layla stared at her blankly. 'I can't be in love. I'm not that sort of person.'

'Trust me, love is indiscriminate. It strikes all types without mercy. I didn't think I was "that sort of person" either and now look at me. I'm someone who has to control everything around them, but take it from me that love can't be controlled. Believe me, I've tried.'

'That's different. You and His Highness knew each other for a long time before you were together. Whereas Raz and I—' Her skin heated as she thought about the intimacies they'd shared. 'We are strangers. We have known each other only a few weeks.'

'I actually find that quite erotic.' Avery leaned back against the arm of the sofa. 'Strangers forced together. I presume you've actually...?' When Layla coloured Avery smiled. 'Mmm, and I'll bet it was good. Raz is super-hot. But don't tell Mal I said that.'

'He was so in love with his wife.' The words fell from Layla's lips before she could stop them and she saw Avery's eyes narrow.

'Yes, and that was tragic. But it happened. Stuff happens.' The laughter had gone and her husky voice hinted at layers of depth beneath the sophisticated social skills. 'It's called life. Sometimes life delivers a steaming pile of crap right in your lap, and when that happens all you can do is keep moving forward. You keep walking. You get out of bed, you move, and eventually you start living again. And that's what he's doing.

'But this marriage wasn't his choice. It was mine.'

'Raz Al Zahki has never done anything that wasn't his choice. He is tough, single-minded and as stubborn as his brother and my husband.' Avery reached across and squeezed her hand. 'And he made a *good* choice. I'm thrilled we're going to be neighbours.'

'I'm nothing like his wife. I can't take her place.'

'Would you want to? Personally, I'd hate to be a clone of another person. You probably don't want my advice, but I'll give it anyway because I can't help myself: don't try and replace her.' Avery unfolded her long legs and slipped on her shoes. 'Be yourself. Be *you*. If you want to learn to ride, then learn. But only if it's what you want to do. You should probably learn to swim, but only so that his psycho sister-in-law can't have the pleasure of drowning you. The point I'm making is that if you are *you* then any relationship you form together will be real.'

Layla felt her mood lift for the first time in days. Maybe even longer. 'That makes sense.'

'Of course it does. I only ever talk sense—as I'm forever telling my husband. Now, drink some tea and tell me about your sister.'

At the mention of her sister Layla felt her happy mood evaporate. 'She's still missing.'

'Yes.' Avery's expression was sympathetic. 'Everyone is looking for her. And Salem is exactly the right person to be in charge of that.'

'Everyone says that, but he didn't look particularly friendly when I saw him.'

'I didn't say he was friendly.' Avery swept a sheet of blonde hair away from her face. 'No, he definitely isn't friendly. Dark. Moody. A bit scary, I suppose. But in a totally hot way. Exactly the right person to find your sister.'

'Why? Why does everyone keep saying that?'

Avery put her cup down carefully. 'You don't know?'

'All I know is that Raz seems to trust his brother with his life.'

'As well he would. Salem isn't just his brother—he's ex-Special Forces. After everything that happened in their family he left to set up his own private security firm. He handles *our* security—although I'm convinced that's just Mal trying to monitor my movements when I'm buying shoes.'

Layla laughed, but her mind was picking over what she now knew of Salem. On that first night he'd stepped in front of his brother to protect him, even though Raz was obviously well able to defend himself. 'He hasn't been in contact.'

'He's a man.' Avery selected a date from the bowl on the table. 'Men never call when they're supposed to, and Salem keeps everything close to his chest. Which isn't a bad place to be, I have to say, because he's all muscle and very sexy.' Catching Layla's expression, she grinned. 'Sorry, I'm trying to cheer you up. I honestly do believe that Salem will find her. He's the best.'

'But if she were alive surely he would have found her by now?'

'Maybe he has. Maybe he's lying low for some reason—such as the fact Hassan is a crackpot and no one knows exactly where he is.' Avery nibbled the date. 'Is she a resilient girl?'

Layla thought about her sister and everything she'd endured. 'Yes.'

'Shy? What would she do if she were picked up by a Bedouin tribe, for example?'

'Talk them to death?'

Avery's brows rose. 'It sounds as if Salem will have his hands full when he finds her. You don't know him, so you'll have to take it from me that he's very serious. And everything he does is top secret so he's not much of a talker.'

'Then how do you know so much about what he does?'

'Just one of the perks of being married to the boss, sweetie.'

Layla sifted through the information at her disposal. 'But if Salem is really as serious as you say he is going to strangle my sister.'

'Yes, it does sound like an interesting match. I predict that she will be a pleasant interruption from his usual life. Now, have some more tea. And eat something. Because it's ages until dinner and I'm always too busy mingling to eat much at these things.'

Avery topped up the cups and Layla breathed deeply.

'I have no idea what is expected of me tonight.'

'You're our guest. All we expect of our guests is that they enjoy themselves. In fact I insist on it or I'll assume my party is a dismal failure.' Seeing the expression on Layla's face, she gave a warm smile. 'Just enjoy the time with Raz. Sounds as if the two of you haven't had much time to get to know each other outside of a crisis situation, so this is a perfect opportunity to explore a whole different side to your relationship.'

'But I knew what was expected of me in the crisis. I knew I had to stop the wedding, find Raz, find my sister—it was stressful, but there was a purpose to it. I don't understand the purpose of a party. That isn't what our relationship is about.'

'Maybe it should be. Maybe you just don't know how to relax because you've never been allowed to. The purpose of tonight,' Avery said, 'is for you to spend time together. Be a couple.'

'I've never been part of a couple. I don't know what I'm doing.' Layla's desperation to talk to someone overrode her natural shyness about the topic. 'Raz is—experienced. I'm worried I'm not the woman he needs.'

Avery stared at her for a long moment and then gave a slow smile that transformed her face from beautiful to pure seductress. Suddenly Layla saw exactly why the Sultan had fallen so hard for her. She was strong and independent, but never at the expense of her femininity.

'Trust me, you are *all* the woman he needs,' Avery said.

Layla gave a helpless shrug. 'I don't know myself anymore. I thought I had such a clear idea of who I was and what I wanted, and then suddenly it turns out I'm wrong.'

'Not wrong, but people change and adapt according to their circumstances.' Avery sipped her tea. 'People grow and learn. Or at least the people worth knowing do. For the record, I'm glad Raz found you. He deserves someone like you. And you deserve him.'

'He was forced to marry me.'

'Stop saying that! Did he marry you kicking and screaming? I didn't think so. Now, finish your tea—we're going to make sure that by the time you and Raz make it back to the bedroom tonight he is going to be a desperate man.'

'I won't be comfortable wearing anything too revealing.'

'Don't worry. The true secret of allure is not to show all but to hint at what you are hiding.'

Layla gave a choked laugh. 'You want him to unwrap me?'

'Well, that's one alternative.' Avery stood up. 'Personally, I have a preference for a scenario where you unwrap yourself and make him watch but not touch. The theme of tonight's ball is Desert Nights. It has so much potential, don't you think?'

CHAPTER TEN

RAZ PACED THE length of the royal rooms that had been allocated to them for their stay and glanced at his watch for the sixth time in as many minutes.

Of Layla there was no sign, and he wondered how she'd coped with being plunged into the centre of a big working palace with people she didn't know. From the little he'd learned about her past he knew she'd had little exposure to glittering social gatherings such as the ones run by the Sultan and his wife. And he'd known Avery long enough to be sure she would have extracted every last scrap of detail from Layla, and suddenly wondered if it had been unfair of him to leave them together for so long.

The Desert Nights Ball—an annual event organised by Avery as a fundraiser for disadvantaged children—was about to begin and their presence was expected.

He pulled out his phone and was about to call Avery when Mal appeared in the doorway of his suite, flanked by his security team.

'I have been sent by my wife to tell you that they will meet us downstairs.'

Raz slid his phone back into his pocket. 'I expected Layla to be here.'

'She's spent the day shopping and lunching with Avery, so expect to find her exhausted.' Mal dismissed his guards with a discreet gesture and walked into the guest suite, closing the door behind him. 'Apparently they want to surprise you. And by that I mean that my wife has taken over, as always. I hope that isn't a problem?'

'I appreciate Avery's help. Layla isn't used to large social gatherings and she's quite shy. I'm worried she'll find it overwhelming.'

Mal gave him a speculative look. 'You care about her?'

'Does that surprise you?'

'Does it surprise *you*?'

'Yes.' Seeing no reason not to be honest with his friend, Raz paced over to the window. 'Yes, it surprises me. She is nothing like I expected her to be. I admit it. I made an assumption about who she was based on what we know about the rest of her family.'

'Most people would have done the same.'

'Perhaps, but it isn't something I'm proud of.' He knew now how desperate things must have been for Layla to choose to ride a strange horse into the desert with no fixed destination. She was careful, cautious—and with reason. Those were the qualities that had kept her alive. 'I suspect her life was hell.'

'Now, that comes as *no* surprise to me.' Mal's voice was hard. 'If you want my honest opinion, she is lucky to now be married to you and is probably feeling nothing but relieved.'

Was she? He realised he knew very little about what she was feeling because she kept her thoughts to herself. Except for that single occasion when she'd lost control and spoken out about the secrets he'd kept from her, she'd made no comment on her new life. He knew that much of what she did was driven by her desire to please him, to compensate in some small way for the sins her father had committed.

'She is very brave. She rides even though she hates it, and although she is scared of the dogs she insists they are allowed to roam free. She refuses to be beaten by fear.'

'Then hopefully it will not be long before she realises that with you there is nothing to fear.'

'I think tonight might be stressful for her.' And he realised he didn't want it to be. He didn't want it to be another task she had to endure, another challenge. He wanted her to relax. He wanted her to have fun and enjoy herself without constantly looking over her shoulder.

Mal was watching him. 'And what about you? This is the first time you have made a public appearance with another woman.'

It was something else that hadn't occurred to him. 'I don't care what people think, but *she* will care.' And people would be speculating about their relationship, his feelings about being married to the daughter of his enemy.

'We will all ensure that she is protected as much as possible. She will receive a warm welcome from all of us and that will help.'

But would that be enough?

'She isn't used to crowds.'

'If you sense she is bothered by it then of course you must leave early,' Mal said immediately. 'No one will be offended. Come up here and spend some time alone. My staff will serve you dinner—anything you need, just ask. You are like a brother to me. I hope you know that.'

Quiet words, but spoken with such sincerity that they unlocked something inside him.

'I do know that. For the past decade you've—'

'You would have done the same for me.' Mal cut him off before he could express his thanks. 'I am glad you've found Layla.'

'She's never danced before. Can you imagine that?' His tone raw, Raz lifted a hand and pressed his fingers to his forehead. 'Her life was *nothing* like I imagined it to be.'

He thought of two small girls, huddled together while they

listened to the dogs approaching. Had an image of the scar on her arm where those dogs had come too close. Knowing how hard it had been for her to share that with him, he had no intention of sharing it with anyone else.

'Having met both her father and Hassan on a few occasions I prefer to forget, I have no trouble believing you.'

'She has no idea how to enjoy herself. I don't think she knows who she really is.'

Mal hesitated and then reached out and squeezed his shoulder. 'Give her time. Her life has changed overnight. She has lived with people she couldn't trust, so it will inevitably take a while for her to realise she can trust *you*. It must be a relief to her to be living with you after the life she has led.'

Was it? He realised that since this whole thing began he'd barely thought further than his own needs. 'I have no idea how she feels about living with me,' Raz said honestly.

Mal raised an eyebrow. 'Don't take this the wrong way, but I think you underestimate your qualities. Not that I claim to be an expert on the minds of women, as my wife is always swift to point out.'

His wry tone made Raz smile. 'Your wife is an amazing woman.'

'She is pregnant.' Mal spoke the words in a rough tone tinged with male pride and then gave a half smile. 'I wasn't supposed to tell anyone that.'

'Congratulations.' It was Raz's turn to reach out. 'I'm pleased for you both.'

'I'd rather you didn't—'

'I won't mention it.'

'Good, because I would be in serious trouble. There will be a public announcement in due course.'

'I shall look suitably surprised.'

Mal glanced towards the door. 'I am the host. I should go downstairs and greet the early arrivals. Join me?'

They walked into the opulent ballroom together and Avery immediately walked up to Raz and kissed him on both cheeks.

'It's good to see you, my friend.'

Dressed in ivory silk, she looked stunning and Raz smiled. 'And it is good to see you. Thank you for looking after Layla.'

'I love her,' Avery said simply. 'She's the kindest, most sweet-natured person. And very, *very* beautiful—but of course you've already noticed that because you're a man. She's nervous, so please say the right thing when you see her. And if you need help working out what that is, don't be afraid to ask.'

Raz didn't respond. He was looking over Avery's shoulder to Layla, who was dressed like something from the *Arabian Nights*. Her dress was midnight-blue shot with silver, high at the neck, cut narrow at the waist. Her hair fell in a smooth sheet, dark as ink over the shimmering fabric. Her beautiful eyes were accentuated by subtle make-up.

'And just in case you're that guy who never asks for help, the word you're looking for is *stunning*,' Avery murmured, and then took Mal's arm and guided him towards the arriving guests, leaving Raz alone with a shimmering, dazzling version of Layla.

She looked at him through the dark sweep of those thick eyelashes that had caught his attention from the first moment he'd seen her.

'Did your meetings go well?'

She sounded composed but he saw the uncertainty in her face and knew that Avery was right about her being nervous.

His mouth on those lips, Raz struggled to focus. 'Very well. And I see you and Avery had a busy afternoon.'

'We had fun. We talked and then we shopped.'

Her eyes sparkled and there was an excitement in her expression he'd ever seen them. It was as if someone had switched on a lightbulb inside her. She had a new confidence.

She carried herself differently. He wondered what had brought about the change.

Was it just the dress?

'You look stunning.'

'She told you to say that. I heard her. But thank you, any-way.'

'I said it because it's true. And I would have done so with-out prompting.' He looked into her eyes and then reached out and drew her against him, his hand resting on the dip of her narrow waist.

'Can I ask you something?'

'Anything.'

'You mentioned dancing—' Her gaze slid to the dance floor, which shimmered and sparkled under clever lighting. 'I'd really like to try it.'

Hiding his surprise, Raz took her hand. 'Then let's try it.'

Intrigued by the change in her, he led her towards the dance floor, exchanging only the briefest of greetings with people as they moved through the crowd, all his attention focused on her.

He noticed Avery in the centre of the dance floor with a man Raz recognised as the French ambassador while Mal was deep in conversation with the man's wife.

When she spotted them Avery immediately escorted the dazzled ambassador back to his wife before grabbing Layla by the hands.

'Don't you *love* this song?' She swirled and shimmied, arms above her head, and Layla watched her curiously for a moment and then joined her, following Avery's lead as she danced, her movements more subtle, more discreet as she learned to match the flow of her body with the beat of the music.

It was a skill that seemed to come naturally too her. Raz felt tension throb through him as he watched her move with sensual grace, her long hair flowing like liquid silk around her shoulders as she discovered a love of dancing. Her happiness at that discovery was evident from the smile on her lips and the unselfconscious way she twirled with Avery, her enjoyment as infectious as the rhythmic beat of the music.

Raz watched her, hypnotised by the change in her, knowing he was witnessing the transformation from unsure girl to sexually aware woman.

Avery caught his eye and gave him a knowing look before twirling Layla into his arms.

She landed against his chest with a gentle thud, off-balance from the dancing and laughing in a way he hadn't heard her laugh before. And he found himself smiling too, because it was impossible not to smile with her eyes sparkling into his and her arms wrapped around his neck as she tried to balance herself.

'I'm dizzy.' Her fingers closed over his biceps. 'Did I embarrass you?'

Was this the first time in her life she'd done something for herself without thought to others? 'No.' His mouth was close to hers, his gaze locked on hers. 'You could never embarrass me.'

By chance, or more likely because the ever-observant Avery had organised it, the rhythm of the music changed from loud and throbbing to soft and smooth and Raz drew her against him, his hand pressed low on her back.

He felt her body relax against his, knew people were watching curiously and tightened his grip on her protectively, hoping she didn't notice the interest and lose that sudden burst of unselfconscious enjoyment that he was finding as addictive as a drug.

Her enchantment with dancing reminded him of that magical moment when a newborn foal staggered to its feet for the first time, balancing on shaky legs as it realised there was a whole new world to explore.

His grip on her must have tightened, because those exotic, beautiful eyes lifted to his in silent question.

Raz felt as if someone had kicked his legs out from under him.

Sexual energy crackled between them, scorching hot and intense. His hand was on her back and he felt the change in her, felt her response to the chemistry as her eyes dropped to his mouth and lingered there.

This time there was no shyness in her gaze, just curiosity, and something far, far more dangerous that came from the knowledge she'd acquired over the past week. Her eyes darkened like the sky before a storm, those eyelashes a silky veil of temptation. And then her lips curved into a happy smile and she leaned her head against his chest, the softness of her hair brushing against his jaw, the scent of it yet another drugging assault on his senses.

Fighting the impulse to drag her from the dance floor, Raz closed his eyes and gathered her close, blocking out everyone around them.

Time passed unobserved until the pace of the music increased and she tilted her head back and looked up at him.

He slid his fingers into her hair, pleased that Avery hadn't suggested she wear it up. 'Do you want to carry on dancing or would you like something to eat? Maybe a drink?'

'The beat has changed.'

'It's a different dance. I can teach you.'

'You must be tired of having to teach me everything.'

Her eyes were soft on his and he tightened his grip on her, pressing her closer until their bodies touched from waist to thigh.

'No, I am not tired of teaching you.' His arm was curved around her and the contours of her body fit perfectly against his. Sexual arousal slammed into him and he felt the answering tremor of her body and knew she felt the same. Her fingers dug into his shoulder. 'You're enjoying yourself?'

'Yes. Very much.'

'Did you have fun with Avery?'

'Yes. I've never talked to another woman before. Not like that.'

'What did you talk about?'

Colour streaked along her cheeks. 'Life.'

'Your life, *habibti*?'

'Not specifically. She talked a bit about you and Salem. She is obviously very fond of you both.'

'Those feelings are returned. Mal has been a friend for as long as I can remember. He and I were at the same party the night he first met Avery. It was like watching two asteroids collide. Everyone in the vicinity was hit by the explosion and the subsequent fallout.' They both glanced towards the edge of the dance floor, where Avery was deep in conversation with Mal, their connection so close it felt like intruding to watch it.

'They're perfect together.'

There was a wistful note in her voice and Raz tilted his head so that he could see her face.

'I thought you weren't romantic?'

Her eyes were fixed across the room on Avery and Mal who were indulging in a last brief exchange before greeting their guests. Remembering what Mal had told him earlier, Raz could guess what the exchange was about.

'I'm not. Not for myself. That doesn't mean I can't be pleased when other people find love.'

He looked down at the glossy curve of Layla's mouth and suddenly wanted to be alone with her, away from the curious glances and the speculation.

'Let's get out of here. The Old Palace is famed for its water gardens. They were a gift from Mal's father to his mother on their marriage.' Keeping his arm around her, he guided her outside.

'Should we be doing this? There are people waiting to speak to you.'

'Then they can wait. I have been doing nothing but speaking to people. Tonight is for us.' He wondered how often before in her life she'd been able to please herself and decided he probably didn't want to hear the answer.

'It's peaceful here.' Tilting her head back, she stared up at the stars. 'I love the sound of the water. It reminds me of your home.'

'*Our* home.'

She hesitated, then pulled away from him and sat down on the low wall that surrounded the bubbling fountain. 'Did your wife love it there? Was it her favourite place?'

He stiffened in instinctive rejection of the personal nature of her question and then saw the anxiety in her eyes and realised how much courage it had taken on her part to ask it. 'Nisa preferred the city. She grew tired of moving around. She was made impatient by the restrictions placed on our movements. She wasn't always careful.'

'I shouldn't have asked.'

But she *had* asked, and emotion settled in his stomach like a solid lump. 'The day she was killed—she wasn't even supposed to be in the desert. She had been staying in the city but had come out to surprise me. I had ridden one of the horses and she climbed into my four-wheel drive. They had tampered with the brakes and she was inexperienced at driving in the desert. Had I been the one at the wheel then perhaps—' He broke off, knowing that 'perhaps' was a useless word. 'She couldn't control the vehicle. It rolled and she was crushed.'

He felt her arms slide round his waist.

'I'm sorry. I'm sorry you lost her. I'm sorry for any part my family played in that. For all of it.'

'An individual is responsible for his own actions. I have never blamed you.' But he understood how hard it must be for her and knew he was the one making it hard.

'It hurts you to talk about it.' Her voice was soft in the semi darkness. 'I apologise. I shouldn't have asked. I've spoiled the moment.'

'You have a right to ask, and you've spoiled nothing.'

'I have no rights, Your Highness. We both know that.'

Sadness shadowed the dark depths of her eyes and Raz pulled her to her feet and took her face in his hands, forcing her to look at him.

'You are still calling me Your Highness after everything we have shared? Have we not moved further on than that?'

'You married me because it was the right thing to do for your people, and in doing so you ignored your personal wishes.'

'Maybe that was true at the time of the wedding, but it isn't true now. Do you think I was ignoring my personal wishes last night? Do you think what we do together has anything to do with my responsibilities?'

'Raz—'

Her hand was on his chest, her eyes on his, and he lowered his head, his mouth hovering above hers.

'Do you think this isn't personal? Does this not feel personal, *habibti*?'

Layla felt everything inside her tighten and spin out of control. Staring into his dangerous black eyes, she felt the world around them fade to nothing. The distant sound of chatter was replaced by the pounding of blood in her ears and her vision was filled with nothing but him.

She felt the roughness of his cheek against the softness of hers, the warmth of his breath and the bite of his strong fingers in her hair as he held her head for his kiss. But he didn't kiss her. Not quite. And the anticipation was electrifying. She felt his tension as powerfully as he evidently felt hers.

'Do we have to stay?' She almost whispered the words. 'Would it be possible to leave?'

His dark brows met in a concerned frown. 'You're not happy? Then we will leave.' Without pressing for further explanation he took her hand and led her towards some steps that led past a cascade of fountains to the rear entrance of the Old Palace. 'We can reach our rooms from here.'

She walked with him through an arched entrance, up spiral stairs, along opulent corridors with gilded mirrors and ornate tapestries, past uniformed staff and the odd exotically clad guest until they reached their private suite.

'I should not have taken you this evening,' he breathed. 'Forgive me.'

'Why do you say that? I had fun. Such fun.'

'You wanted to leave.'

'But not because I wasn't enjoying myself.'

'Then why?'

Layla hesitated, and then stepped forward and placed her hands on his chest. 'Because of this. Because of what I want to do.' She felt him tense. Saw the shock in his eyes as he realised her reasons for abandoning the party were not the ones he'd assumed they were.

'Layla—'

'Don't speak.' She wanted the illusion. No matter what lay between them, tonight it was all about the chemistry and she didn't want to shatter that with words. Whatever emotional hurdles they faced, physically there were none.

This time her fingers were swift and sure as she undressed him. Within seconds he was naked from the waist up, his trousers riding low on his waist, revealing a gloriously masculine chest, every line of muscle clearly delineated as he stood in front of her. Her fingers slid up his chest to his shoulders and then lingered on the hard swell of his biceps. His physical strength fascinated her, and she traced the shape of his muscles with the tips of her fingers, hearing his breathing change, feeling the tension in him as he held himself still and let her explore. She took her time because she wanted to discover and memorise every inch of him. After her fingers she used her lips, her tongue retracing the line her fingers had taken. And still he stood still, although she sensed the effort it took him to do so.

Candles flickered in all corners of the room, sending shafts of shimmering light across them, turning his chest from bronze to gold.

Without hesitation she undid his trousers and dropped to her knees in front of him, her hair falling in a sweep of dark silk over her shoulders.

She glanced up at him and his gaze clashed with hers and held.

Then slowly, gently, she took him in her mouth and saw his eyes close, his jaw clench. She felt the thickness of him in her mouth, tasted the silky, salty heat of him, until he groaned deep in his throat and closed his hands in her hair, easing her away from him.

'Give me a minute—'

His voice was thickened, his eyes dark with something she hadn't seen before, and then he pulled her to her feet and their mouths came together at the same time. This time there was nothing gentle about the kiss, no tentative exploration or patient instruction, just raw, undiluted passion. His hands were locked in her hair and then ripping at her dress as they kissed, so hungry for each other they staggered slightly and sent a lamp flying from its place on a table.

Raz caught it in his hand and she laughed against his mouth. 'Good catch, Your Highness.'

'If it had fallen we would have had Security swarming all over this place.'

Without lifting his mouth from hers he replaced the lamp and urged her back towards the bed, but Layla twisted at the last moment so that this time he was the one on his back on the bed and she was the one on top.

Her hair fell forward onto his chest and he slid his fingers into it.

'I love your hair.'

Smiling, she licked her way down his chest, heard him groan deep in his throat as she moved lower again, exploring him intimately, until his hands closed on her hips and he shifted her over him, his impatience evident in the hard bite of his fingers.

His hair-roughened thigh brushed against the softness of hers and she lowered herself onto him, watching his eyes turn deep, dark black as he drove deep into her. Layla moaned with the sheer pleasure of it, moving instinctively, until he locked his fingers over her hips to control her movements.

'Give me a minute—'

His tone was raw, right on the edge of control, and she leaned forward to kiss his mouth, licking at his lips until he muttered something unintelligible and caught her head in his hands. They kissed like wild things, the heat a pulsing, pounding force, his body hard in hers as they drove each other to the same peak and over the edge. She felt him pulse inside her, watched his face as he lost control, as pleasure gripped them both and spun them into ecstasy.

Afterwards, she curled against his chest and felt his hand come up to touch her hair.

He didn't speak and neither did she, because she'd learned how easily words could destroy and she wanted to preserve the moment. Preferably forever, but if not forever then at least for now.

And in the aftermath of their loving, while they both lay bathed in intimacy, she knew that Avery had been right.

She loved him.

The realisation was overwhelming, terrifying and puzzling all at the same time.

But most of all it was shocking. Shocking to learn yet another thing about herself. When she'd made the decision that marriage to Raz was the best solution, she'd braced herself for living with a stranger, but she was fast discovering that the stranger she was living with was herself.

She realised that her life before him had been as dry and empty as the vast desert. Because she'd never known anything else she'd assumed that was all there was, but now she knew differently. She'd thought she knew herself well, but had discovered she'd only known one small part of herself. And as for knowing *him*—

They say his heart is frozen into ice.

She knew that wasn't true.

She lifted her head and looked at him, staring down into the fierce black of his eyes. To describe him as handsome was to do him a disservice, because his appeal went so much deeper than that. Etched in those striking features was a strength that was more than surface deep.

Something flickered in those ebony depths and she saw all her own questions reflected back at her.

Without speaking he lifted his hand and pushed her hair away from her face. It was impossible not to react to his touch because it seemed everything she felt about this man was exaggerated and out of her control.

She felt a stab of envy for his wife, whom he had loved so deeply, swiftly followed by guilt that she could feel that way about someone no longer alive.

A few weeks ago she hadn't known anything about love.

She'd felt disconnected from the poets' description of the

agony and heartache that came with love and loss. She'd never seen any evidence to support the theory that hearts could break, shatter or be frozen into ice.

She'd been willing to believe in love, but had never expected to experience the reality.

But now she had both experience and evidence. She felt the pain of it heavy in her chest, the ache behind her ribcage growing by the hour.

Raz frowned slightly and just for a moment she thought he was going to say something. Then he gathered her close and pulled the covers over them both.

'That was amazing. *You* are amazing.'

Layla said nothing because she had no idea what to say.

When she'd made the decision to suggest marriage to him she'd been prepared to live in a loveless partnership. Any alternative hadn't occurred to her, because although she'd been willing to believe love existed for other people she'd had no evidence to suggest she was capable of it. All she'd wanted was respect and kindness. She'd been ignorant of the impact of sexual attraction and ignorant of the power of love.

But now she knew about both.

And she knew love hurt.

'Do you have to go away, Daddy?'

Raz turned at the sound of his daughter's voice and saw her standing watching him, her expression forlorn. Layla hurried towards her, trying to distract the little girl with the promise of a swim.

Raz noticed she didn't look at him.

It had been two weeks since the party in Zubran, and since their return Layla had been withdrawn and quiet. So quiet he was becoming increasingly concerned.

He made a mental note to talk to her about it immediately on his return.

'I have to go, but it's only for one night.' He scooped Zahra into his arms. 'When I come back we will ride together, I promise.'

As if realising that she should say something, Layla roused herself. 'Where are you going?'

'I have another meeting with the Tazkhan Council—this time to discuss arrangements for formalising my position.'

'So will we be moving to the city?'

It was Zahra who asked the question, but he wondered if that was what was bothering Layla.

'We will live there for some of the time, but not all.' He watched Layla's face but her expression didn't change.

As his security guards made the final preparations around him he drew Layla to one side. 'You are very quiet. Is something worrying you?'

'Nothing. I hope your meeting goes well.'

She was detached and formal and he knew this wasn't the right time to push her. Not with his daughter watching and his security team hovering in the background.

'I will be back tomorrow.' He lifted his hand to her face, intending to kiss her, and then let his hand drop, shocked by the impulse. They were in public, their exchange witnessed by a dozen other people.

Before he could say anything she stepped back. 'Safe trip.'

CHAPTER ELEVEN

LAYLA LAY AWAKE in the bed, sleep chased away by the ache in her chest.

Maybe a heart *could* break.

She'd read about people who lost partners only to die themselves.

Maybe such a thing was possible. Just one more thing she'd been wrong about.

It was almost a relief that Raz was away for a night because she didn't know how to be with him any more. She didn't know how *not* to show him that she loved him, and she didn't know how to stop herself falling harder and deeper.

Unable to sleep, she decided to read for a while and pressed the switch for the light by the bed. Nothing happened. Assuming the bulb had blown, she leaned across and tried the other one. When that didn't work either she pulled on a robe, slid on her shoes and walked out of her bedroom and onto the terrace. Stars twinkled in the sky and everything was quiet.

Too quiet.

Lights should have been burning in the house and outside on the terrace, but everything was in darkness and the fountain was silent. There was no sound of running water, no sounds at all.

It was eerily quiet.

Layla wondered if there had been a power cut and was

about to go back to her room and find a torch when she realised that there were no security guards outside Zahra's room.

Her heart stopped and she ceased to breathe for a few seconds.

No lights. No guards.

Grateful that there was enough moonlight for her to see the way, she walked quickly to Zahra's bedroom, adjacent to hers. There was sufficient light for her to see Isis and Horus curled up on the bed next to the little girl, and for once she was relieved to see them.

Her heart was pounding hard and her hands were clammy, and she stood for a moment, trying to rationalize the situation. The most likely explanation was a blown fuse or some other electrical fault.

Was she overreacting?

Possibly, but all she could hear in her head were Raz's words.

Show me the evidence that my daughter would have been safe.

She didn't have evidence, and she knew better than to underestimate Hassan at any time—least of all now, when he was likely to be at his most desperate.

What if he had somehow discovered that Raz had a daughter?

What if he decided to use that fact?

No matter that she might be overreacting. She couldn't risk letting Raz lose someone else he loved.

'Zahra…' Keeping her voice soft, she reached out a hand towards the sleeping child.

Isis opened one eye and looked at her.

Keeping as far away from the dogs as possible, Layla gave Zahra a gentle shake. 'Wake up. We're going on an adventure.'

Zahra snuggled under the covers. 'It's dark.'

'I know. The dark is going to make it extra exciting. We're going to have fun.'

The child yawned sleepily. 'Where are we going?'

Where? It was a good question.

For a moment Layla's mind blanked, and then she knew exactly what she had to do. Something she'd done many times before. 'We're going to play a game called Hide.' Her mouth dried at the memory, because those games, too, had been played in the dark. Pulling back the covers, she tugged the little girl into her arms, trying desperately not to frighten her. 'We'll just put on your coat in case it gets cold.'

'It's night-time. Why are we playing a game at night-time?'

'That's the best time to play it. I used to play it with my sister when she was your age. There are rules.' She manoeuvred Zahra into the coat. 'First, you mustn't make a sound. Second, you have to do exactly as I say. If I tell you to keep still you have to keep still. If I tell you to run you have to run.'

'This game sounds like fun, but why can't we play it to-morrow?'

Layla caught a flash of light out of the corner of her eye and saw lights approaching in the distance. Torches? Headlights?

Sure now that the threat was real, she cuddled the little girl close. 'Because it's going to be more fun to play it now. We have to go.'

Still sleepy, Zahra glanced back at the bed. 'Can Isis and Horus come too?'

Already halfway to the door, Layla eyed the dogs, watching her from the bed. 'Yes. Good idea. But we have to move quickly.'

Zahra called the dogs and they bounded across the bedroom. 'But who are we hiding from, Layla? What's the point of playing Hide if no one is going to try and find us?'

'We will find a safe place and see how still and silent we

can be. We're going to practise and then, when we're really, really good at it, Daddy can play it with us when he comes home.' Layla knew she was making no sense, and she was so afraid she could hardly make her legs move. Half walking, half running, she kept chatting and pretending it was all a game, trying not to frighten Zahra.

Because she knew now that they were being hunted.

She *felt* it, and the terror rushed over her as familiar and terrifying as it had been when she was a child.

'Zahra, listen to me.' It was a struggle to keep her voice light. 'If you didn't want anyone to find you where would you go? Where is the *best* hiding place around here?'

'Dahl Al Zahki. The Desert Caves.'

Layla had a dim memory of Raz pointing them out to her on a ride earlier in the week. 'Are they close?'

'We can ride there in five minutes.'

Ride.

Layla closed her eyes and faced the inevitable. 'Let's do it.'

'If you really want to be fast we should take Raja.'

'Your father's stallion?'

'I can ride him. You can just hold onto me. I *like* this game.' Zahra was wide awake now and bouncing in her arms. 'I'm glad you woke me up.'

They reached the stables and Layla turned and again saw the flash of lights in the distance. *How long did they have?* 'We'll take Raja. It's a great idea. But how will we find the way?'

'I know the way and so does he. He was born here. My daddy had him from a foal. But you'll have to help me up because he's too big.'

Somehow Layla managed to get both of them on the enormous horse and Zahra giggled.

'His coat feels all warm on my legs. I've never ridden in my nightie before.'

Layla pulled the coat round the child and resisted the temptation to look down. It felt as if her life had come full circle. She'd begun this new chapter by stealing her father's stallion and riding it into the desert, and now she was ending it in a similar way. Only this time she was determined not to fall.

'Go, Zahra. Get us out of here.'

'You've never galloped before.'

'Then it's time I learned and I know you'll be the perfect teacher. Isis—Horus—' she hissed their names '—come.'

The stallion sprang forward, needing no encouragement to unleash all that restrained power. Layla's breath caught and then she was hanging on, trying to remember everything Raz and Abdul had taught her about relaxing into the rhythm.

It was the most terrifying, uncomfortable few minutes of her life, but with each long, pounding stride she knew they were drawing away from whoever was at the other end of the light, so she concentrated on not falling off and let Zahra do the rest.

'We're here.'

They arrived at the caves and Layla slid off the horse, landing with an uncomfortable thud on the uneven ground. Zahra slid into her arms and the dogs stayed close. 'We need to get inside.'

'No. We have to tie Raja up or he could wander off and Daddy will be angry.'

'We'll take him with us deeper into the caves. We need to be out of sight.'

She shone her torch once and saw several tunnels leading off the main cavern. 'Over there—that's a good place to hide.'

'Why are you so good at finding hiding places?'

'Because I used to play this game with my little sister when she was your age.'

But she'd made a cardinal mistake. The horse had provided a quick escape vehicle, but by bringing the animal there was no way they could disguise their presence. 'We have to let Raja loose, Zahra. We *have* to.'

With luck the people tracking them would follow the horse, thinking they were still together.

'No! We can't do that. Daddy will be angry.'

'I'll take the blame. I'll tell him it's all my fault. But we have to let him go.'

'No! I won't let you—'

But Layla had already removed the reins and given the enormous stallion a slap on the rump. Delighted to be free of his reins, Raja launched himself into the darkness while Zahra gave a sob.

'He will hurt himself. He'll—'

'He's going to be fine.' Layla grabbed the child in her arms and sprinted across the cave. Zahra was squirming so badly she almost dropped her.

'But, Layla, he doesn't—'

'Hush.' Layla slammed her hand over the child's mouth and pulled her behind the rocks. 'I can hear someone coming. Don't be frightened, but do not make a sound. Not a sound. Isis—Horus—*down*.' The dogs slunk behind the rock obediently and lay down with them just seconds before lights shone into the cave.

'Don't be scared,' Layla whispered, holding Zahra tightly in her arms. 'I've got you.'

'They cannot both have vanished.'

It was Hassan's voice, speaking the same words he'd spoken the night she'd last seen him. Layla closed her eyes, back in her father's bedroom on the night of his death, only this time the person she was protecting was Raz al Zahki's child.

She hugged Zahra against her, keeping her hand over her mouth as she had done so many times with her sister, and all the time she was wondering how Hassan could possibly have known they were here. How had he even found out about Zahra's existence?

'They have to be here. There is nowhere else they could have hidden.'

Recognising Nadia's voice, Layla felt shock punch through her.

So now she had her answer.

She felt Zahra wriggle and held her tighter, but the sudden movement had dislodged something and sent stones tumbling, the sound magnified by the cavernous walls of their hiding place.

Layla realised she had nothing with which to defend them both. No knife. No weapon of any sort with which to protect Raz's child.

'Stay there, and whatever happens don't move.' Whispering the words, she stood up and moved out from behind the rock just as torchlight swept across the cave and dazzled her eyes.

'It's *her*.' Nadia's voice was thickened with contempt. 'If she's here then the child will be with her.'

'Zahra is asleep in her bed. I left her there when I ran. I assumed it was me you wanted. Well, here I am.' Layla walked forward and saw the glint of Nadia's eyes.

'She's lying. She's never far from the girl because she thinks that's the way to get Raz to love her.'

Before Layla could respond Hassan stepped into the beam of light. She felt a shiver run down her body from neck to toes as she remembered all the occasions he'd stood over her trembling body when she'd run from him as a child.

Determined that Zahra wasn't going to know that same fear, she stood as tall as she could. But he simply smiled.

'The best way to look for something is to hunt it and I know just how to do that.'

He snapped his fingers and before Layla could work out

what he was doing she heard the sound of panting and four Saluki shot into the cave towards her.

Her knees liquid, she stumbled back towards Zahra, determined to protect her, the terror so acute she could hardly walk.

She should have anticipated that he'd use Saluki.

She could hear the dull thud of their paws as they raced across the cave towards her, heard the sharp patter of stones dislodged, the low whine and the panting of the dogs as they drew closer. And then she was on her knees beside Zahra, shielding her, covering her, determined to protect her even if it meant the flesh was torn from her bones.

She braced herself for the feel of hot breath on her neck and then pain, but the growling intensified and Isis and Horus sprang in front of them. And then there was nothing but the most terrifying snarling as the dogs clashed, swirling together in the darkness in some macabre dance that sent dust and fur flying.

'Isis!'

Horrified, Zahra tried to go to them, but Layla held her tightly, wondering helplessly how two dogs could possibly be a match against four. And even if she'd wanted to help she couldn't, because the dogs were wild as they fought each other and she couldn't make out Isis and Horus from Hassan's beasts. The best she could do was take advantage of the distraction.

'Is there another way out of these caves?' She spoke the words urgently but the little girl shook her head.

'Not without ropes.'

It wasn't the news Layla wanted, but just as she was about to carry Zahra deeper into the caves there was the sound of vehicles approaching at speed. The next moment the whole cavern was filled with light and there were shouts and something that sounded like gunfire.

Layla flattened Zahra down on the ground.

The snarling became a whimper.

And then she heard the harsh tones of Raz's voice and knew that the guns and the lights belonged to his security team. Almost melting with relief that she was no longer alone, she snuggled Zahra close, afraid to move until she was sure it was safe.

All around them was pandemonium. Layla kept low, knowing that the best thing she could do was not make the situation more dangerous by moving around.

'Layla? *Layla!*' His voice was raw and desperate, the emotion painful to hear, and she knew she had to reassure him.

'It's fine,' she called out. 'She's safe. She's here with me. They haven't touched her.'

Before she could stop her Zahra wriggled out from under her and started to run towards her father, but then she stopped dead.

'Isis? *Isis!*'

Layla saw that the dog was lying still, her blonde fur coated in blood, while Horus stood guard over her body, a sombre sentinel.

'Oh, no—' Layla ran towards Zahra but the little girl was already on her knees beside the dog, sobs tearing through her chest as she tried to cuddle her.

'Don't die, Isis. Daddy, don't let Isis die. Please *do something.*' She scooped the dog's head onto her lap, stroking, rocking, making a terrible keening sound.

Her distress was so painful to witness Layla felt tears on her own cheeks. She reached the child at the same time as Raz.

'Let me look at her.'

His voice was calm and steady, but Layla noticed that his fingers shook slightly as he gently examined the dog. He snapped a command over his shoulder and someone appeared with a flashlight so that he could take a closer look.

'She's been bitten. We need to stop this bleeding.'

'Here—' Layla ripped off the cord that was holding her robe together and dropped to her knees beside him. 'Make a tourniquet. That should do until we can get her back home.'

Her hands were over his and together they tied it firmly and then tightened it. It was the first time she'd touched a dog voluntarily, but she didn't even think about it until she felt something cold and damp nudge her palm and saw Horus standing next to her, looking at her with anxious eyes.

'Good boy.' Layla hesitated and then reached out and stroked his head. 'She's going to be all right.'

'No, she isn't. They saved us from that bad man,' Zahra sobbed, 'and now Isis is going to die.'

'She is *not* going to die.' Delivering a series of orders, Raz rose to his feet in a fluid movement and peeled his daughter away from her beloved pet. 'But we have to get her help, *habibti*. We have to get her home right now. And you need to come home, too. You need to be brave and put your trust in others.'

Zahra clung to him, her little body shuddering with sobs, and Layla rubbed the tears from her own cheeks so that she could help as Raz's men gently lifted Isis and took her limp body to the nearest vehicle, accompanied by a worried Horus who refused to leave her side.

Layla turned to Raz. 'Where is Hassan?'

'He has been arrested, along with Nadia, who apparently masterminded tonight's episode. They are both being taken to Tazkhan for questioning.'

Layla stared at him, still stunned by the discovery that Nadia had been involved. 'I assumed Hassan had forced her in some way. Why would she do that?'

'Jealousy.' Raz's mouth was grim. 'She was jealous of her sister. Apparently she had some deluded idea that I'd marry *her*. It is something I only discovered in the past few hours.

It explains so much about her behaviour and I am angry with myself for not seeing it sooner.'

'Why would you?' Layla shivered and rubbed Zahra's back gently. 'We need to get her home.'

His gaze lingered on hers. 'How can I ever thank you?'

'You don't need to thank me.'

Raz inhaled deeply. 'There is much I need to say to you.'

Layla was too exhausted to contemplate a conversation. 'It can all wait.'

'The vet says Isis will make a good recovery and Zahra is finally asleep.' His handsome face drawn and tired, Raz walked across the bedroom. 'I have put a mattress next to the dog and both Abdul and Horus are sleeping with her for now, along with four of my security team. It's like a menagerie down there. All I need is for Raja to join them and the circus that is our life will be complete.'

The fact that he'd said 'our' warmed her, as did the wry humour in his voice, but Layla wasn't fooled. She knew how raw he was feeling because she felt the same way. She was still so shocked by everything that had happened she felt disconnected.

The warm sunshine and the soothing sound of the fountain in the courtyard beyond the doors to their bedroom were a contrast to the long, terrifying hours of the night before.

Knowing that she wouldn't be able to rest, she'd taken a hot shower, scrubbed away the physical evidence of their flight through the desert and changed into a practical outfit of trousers and a loose shirt, intending to go and sit with Isis and Zahra.

'I'm so relieved Raja is all right. Zahra was beside herself when I turned him loose, but at that point I was still hoping they wouldn't find us. I'm sorry. I didn't know what else to do.'

'You did the right thing. I still can't believe you rode my

stallion.' Raz shook his head and looked at her in naked disbelief. 'How did you do that?'

'I didn't. I just sat on him. It was Zahra who rode him. It's
a good thing she takes after you.'

There was a glint of anger in his eyes. 'They arranged for
me to be away last night. They arranged for you to be alone.
If you hadn't woken—' He raked his hand through his hair,
visibly tense. 'Why did you? Did you hear something? Did
they disturb you?'

'No. I wasn't asleep.' She didn't tell him she'd been lying
there thinking about him. 'I turned the light on to read and
nothing happened. At first I thought it was the bulb and then
I realised the whole place was dark and there were no guards.
Just like that night—' Realisation dawned and she felt the
colour drain from her face. 'Just like that night in the desert
a few weeks ago.'

'Yes. That was to have been their first attempt to take my
daughter and use her as leverage against me, but you foiled
that one, too, by climbing into bed with her. They didn't anticipate that. They weren't prepared for the two of you. But
this time they were.'

'How did you find out?'

'I arrived in Tazkhan and had an illuminating conversation
with the senior council members, all of whom were surprised
by my arrival. As soon as I realised what had happened I returned as quickly as I could, but I was terrified I was going to
be too late.' He pulled her into his arms. 'You were so brave.
You took my daughter into the desert and you took the dogs
with you, and I know how much you fear them.'

'Not any more. I took them because I thought they might
protect Zahra and they did. They were unbelievably brave.'
She shivered as she relived those awful moments. 'I didn't
know how two could possibly win a fight against four, but
now I do. Isis and Horus love her so much they would have

died for her, and that love gave them ten times the strength of Hassan's dogs. I've never seen anything like it.' Remembering moved her so much that tears sprang into her eyes and spilled onto her cheeks. 'Sorry—I think I'm just very tired.' Embarrassed by her loss of control, she lifted her hand to brush them away, but he was there before her, his fingers gentle as he stroked away her tears.

'You must be exhausted, and *so* stressed after everything that has happened.'

'I'm just relieved. And worried about poor Isis.'

'I am assured by the vet that she is going to be fine. And, on the subject of being fine, I have good news about your sister. Salem contacted me half an hour ago, when we were with Isis. He has Yasmin safe.'

'Really?' The tears still flowed and Layla wondered what on earth the matter was with her that she couldn't get through five minutes without crying. 'You're sure? It's really her?'

'Salem says he has never met a woman who talks as much as she does.'

'Then it's *definitely* her.' Layla was laughing with relief and happiness as she hugged Raz. 'Thank you. You were right to have faith in your brother.'

'So now we have your sister safe, Hassan and Nadia off the scene and Isis recovering, perhaps we can finally focus on our own relationship, *habibti*. There are things I must say to you.'

Not now.

She kept her face pressed to his chest so that he couldn't see the change in her expression. She couldn't cope with any more trauma in one night. *Couldn't cope with hearing him tell her again that he couldn't ever love another woman.*

'There is nothing to say. And we ought to check on Zahra—'

'Zahra is fine for the moment.' He eased her away from him so that she was forced to look at him. 'I have never felt fear as I felt it tonight.'

Hearing the change in his voice, Layla pushed down her own feelings. It was selfish of her to think of herself when he was also in shock. 'It must have been terrible for you, being so afraid for your daughter.'

'I wasn't only afraid for my daughter.' He took her face in his hands and the expression in his eyes made her catch her breath.

'Raz—'

'*Don't* speak.' He covered her mouth with his fingers. 'There are things I have to say and I need to say them without interruption. I owe you an apology.' His words thickened. 'You came to me that night in the desert and I was cold, distant and uncaring. I was *so* hard on you and it shames me to remember it.'

'It shouldn't. I thought your behaviour was very restrained in the circumstances.'

'I should have asked more questions that night. I should have suspected that you had suffered great trauma. But I looked no deeper than the surface and I cannot forgive myself for that.'

'I probably wouldn't have told you even had you asked,' Layla mumbled. 'And you behaved very decently towards me, given everything my family has done to yours.'

'I pride myself on being fair and treating everyone as an individual. You are not responsible for the sins of your family.'

'But you didn't know that. Given everything that had happened, you would have been less than human had you not had reservations about me. You were protecting your family and you would not be the man you are had you not done that. It's one of the things I love about you.' The words slipped out without thought and she saw his eyes darken. 'Respect and admire you,' she said quickly. 'I meant that it is one of the things I respect and admire about you.'

'*Is* that what you meant?'

'Yes.' Trapped, she averted her head, but he caught her chin in his fingers and gently forced her to look at him. 'Raz—'

'You were the one who insisted on honesty in this relationship. You've never been afraid to tell me the truth before. You weren't afraid to tell me I was wrong to trust Nadia and that I shouldn't have kept my daughter's existence a secret from you. You weren't afraid to ask about Nisa, even though most people dare not broach that subject with me. Why would you be afraid to tell me the truth about your feelings?'

Why? Because she wasn't sure she could handle his response.

'Feelings were never part of the deal when we married.'

'That is true. But life does not stand still—as we have both discovered. People change. Feelings change. Pain we believe we cannot endure we somehow learn to live alongside. Although I am pleased to have your respect and your admiration, I would so much rather have the first thing you were offering, *habibti.*' His voice husky, he looked down into her eyes. 'Tell me why you were awake last night. The truth.'

'I couldn't sleep.'

'*Why* couldn't you sleep?'

It was clear he wasn't going to let it drop so Layla gave up, too wrung out to keep fighting him.

'Because I missed you. Because I *love* you—' It was a surprising relief to say it. A relief to finally acknowledge the emotions she'd been holding back. 'I love you. I didn't expect to, I didn't think I could, but I do. And I wouldn't have told you except that you forced the subject, and I hope it doesn't make things awkward because it really shouldn't.'

'Why would it make things awkward?'

Wasn't it obvious?

'Because I know you're not capable of loving another woman. Our marriage was driven by political necessity. We both know that.'

'It is true that it began that way, but sometimes it is less important how something begins, *habibti*, than how it ends.'

Ends?

It was shocking how quickly happiness could turn to misery. 'You want to end it?'

'No! I do *not* want to end it. Not ever. I'm trying to tell you that things have changed. Everything has changed. Including my feelings.' His tone raw, he hauled her against him. 'This is the most important conversation of my life and I'm making a mess of it. I'm *trying* to tell you I love you, too.'

Layla was pressed against him and she could feel the strong thud of his heart against her cheek.

His heart not frozen into ice but warm, healthy and capable of love.

Heat spread through her, driving away the chill that had been part of her since her flight through the desert.

Raz eased her away from him so that he could see her face. 'I loved Nisa. That is a fact and it will never change. We met as children—grew up together.' He frowned slightly, as if he'd never thought much about it before. 'She was always part of my life. I don't even remember either one of us making the decision to marry—it felt inevitable. And then when I lost her—'

Layla slid her arms round him, feeling his pain as her own. 'You honestly don't have to talk about this.'

'I want to. Since I met you it's been easier to talk about it. I was trapped in my old life, clinging to memories because moving on without her felt too hard. And then I met you.'

'That first night—'

'I felt guilty.' His voice was soft. 'It felt like a betrayal. Not just because I was with you, but because that night was so special. I didn't anticipate that what we shared would be so powerful. I rejected it precisely because the chemistry between us was so intense, *habibti*. I'd expected to feel nothing. Instead I felt deeply, and I didn't know how to handle those feelings.'

'I didn't expect you to love me. I didn't expect to love *you*,' Layla confessed honestly. 'I've never loved anyone except my sister. I've never looked at a man and felt anything until that night I met you for the first time. I'd never met a man like you. I'd never met a man who used his strength and power for good rather than personal gain.'

'You were so brave, arriving with nothing but two books.'

His eyes gleamed and she felt the colour darken her cheeks.

'You've taught me everything. It would have been nice to bring something to this marriage and teach you something in return.'

'You have.' Lifting his hand, he touched her cheek. 'You've taught me that life does not stand still. That love can come from unexpected places. That there is always hope. And you've taught me to love again, *habibti*. When you came to me I was so closed off. I couldn't even think about allow-ing another woman into my life. But instead of putting on pressure you just accepted me as I was and didn't try and change that.'

'I wouldn't want to change it. I know you loved Nisa.'

'Yes, but I've learned that loving you doesn't diminish what I felt for her. It took me a while to accept my feelings for you without guilt. She was part of my past, but you are my future. I consider myself fortunate to have fallen in love twice in a lifetime when many do not ever find themselves in possession of that gift.'

Layla swallowed. 'I didn't think I would. I didn't grow up with expectations of love and happy endings. It just wasn't what I thought about. When I came to you in the desert that night I wasn't thinking about love. All I wanted from this marriage was your respect. I used you as an escape from the life I had and because I knew that without me Hassan could not rule, and he is not a man who should be in a position of power. I didn't expect anything else. I didn't expect you to notice so much about me and be so caring. You think you were hard on me, but there were so many times when you tried to make life easier for me. You noticed I was scared of the dogs and tried to keep them away from me—' She choked slightly. 'No one has ever done anything like that for me before. No one has *ever* wanted to protect me.'

'I never cease to be impressed by your determination to confront everything you fear. Particularly riding my stallion!'

'He was remarkably tolerant. I wonder if he somehow knew he was part of our escape.' Layla gave a half smile. 'And Isis and Horus came too.'

'All your nightmares in one evening,' Raz said dryly, but his hand was gentle as he stroked her cheek. 'You are an example to all of us, *habibti.*

'My biggest nightmare was that something might happen to Zahra. I love her, too. She is so confident and trusting, and I hated the thought of that confidence and trust being crushed.'

'She told me you turned the whole thing into a game so that she wouldn't be scared.' He hesitated. 'When I saw her a moment ago she asked me if she is allowed to call you Mummy.'

'Oh—' Emotion wedged itself in her throat. 'But you—'

'One of the biggest sources of my guilt—and believe me there are many—is the fact that I told you not to think of yourself as my daughter's mother.' His handsome face was paler than usual. 'It was a terrible thing to say. I hope you will forgive me.'

'There's nothing to forgive. You were in the most awful situation, being forced to marry me and—' Layla broke off, her vision blurred by tears. 'Do you know what I think? I think I like what you said just now, about separating the past and the future. Can we do that? And if Zahra is thinking of me as her mother then the future is looking better all the time.'

He hauled her close. 'I didn't think I would ever feel this happy. I didn't think it was possible.'

'Me neither.' She hugged him tightly, feeling happier than she ever had in her life before. 'I love you. I love you so much.'

Raz slid his hand into her hair, his mouth close to hers. 'I will never tire of hearing you say that.'

'It was Avery who noticed the way I felt about you.'

The corners of his mouth flickered into a smile. 'Avery is a master at interfering in the lives of others.'

'But in a good way. She was the one who encouraged me to just be myself. I was very confused. I knew I loved you and I didn't know how to live with those feelings without sharing them with you. I didn't know how to be with you. She was the one who pointed out that I should be myself. Just me. That you deserved to know the real me.'

'And I fell in love with the real you.'

Raz lowered his forehead to hers and she slid her arms around his neck, dizzy with the feelings inside her.

'Could you say that again? Just one more time? I need to keep hearing it.'

'I will be saying it many times. I love you. I will love you forever and always,' he breathed, gathering her against him. '*Enti hayati*. You are my life, *habibti*.'

* * * * *

Mills & Boon® Hardback

September 2013

ROMANCE

Challenging Dante	Lynne Graham
Captivated by Her Innocence	Kim Lawrence
Lost to the Desert Warrior	Sarah Morgan
His Unexpected Legacy	Chantelle Shaw
Never Say No to a Caffarelli	Melanie Milburne
His Ring Is Not Enough	Maisey Yates
A Reputation to Uphold	Victoria Parker
A Whisper of Disgrace	Sharon Kendrick
If You Can't Stand the Heat...	Joss Wood
Maid of Dishonour	Heidi Rice
Bound by a Baby	Kate Hardy
In the Line of Duty	Ami Weaver
Patchwork Family in the Outback	Soraya Lane
Stranded with the Tycoon	Sophie Pembroke
The Rebound Guy	Fiona Harper
Greek for Beginners	Jackie Braun
A Child to Heal Their Hearts	Dianne Drake
Sheltered by Her Top-Notch Boss	Joanna Neil

MEDICAL

The Wife He Never Forgot	Anne Fraser
The Lone Wolf's Craving	Tina Beckett
Re-awakening His Shy Nurse	Annie Claydon
Safe in His Hands	Amy Ruttan

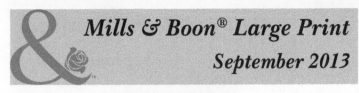

Mills & Boon® Large Print
September 2013

ROMANCE

A Rich Man's Whim	Lynne Graham
A Price Worth Paying?	Trish Morey
A Touch of Notoriety	Carole Mortimer
The Secret Casella Baby	Cathy Williams
Maid for Montero	Kim Lawrence
Captive in his Castle	Chantelle Shaw
Heir to a Dark Inheritance	Maisey Yates
Anything but Vanilla...	Liz Fielding
A Father for Her Triplets	Susan Meier
Second Chance with the Rebel	Cara Colter
First Comes Baby...	Michelle Douglas

HISTORICAL

The Greatest of Sins	Christine Merrill
Tarnished Amongst the Ton	Louise Allen
The Beauty Within	Marguerite Kaye
The Devil Claims a Wife	Helen Dickson
The Scarred Earl	Elizabeth Beacon

MEDICAL

NYC Angels: Redeeming The Playboy	Carol Marinelli
NYC Angels: Heiress's Baby Scandal	Janice Lynn
St Piran's: The Wedding!	Alison Roberts
Sydney Harbour Hospital: Evie's Bombshell	Amy Andrews
The Prince Who Charmed Her	Fiona McArthur
His Hidden American Beauty	Connie Cox

0813 GEN STD LP

Mills & Boon® Hardback

October 2013

ROMANCE

The Greek's Marriage Bargain	Sharon Kendrick
An Enticing Debt to Pay	Annie West
The Playboy of Puerto Banús	Carol Marinelli
Marriage Made of Secrets	Maya Blake
Never Underestimate a Caffarelli	Melanie Milburne
The Divorce Party	Jennifer Hayward
A Hint of Scandal	Tara Pammi
A Façade to Shatter	Lynn Raye Harris
Whose Bed Is It Anyway?	Natalie Anderson
Last Groom Standing	Kimberly Lang
Single Dad's Christmas Miracle	Susan Meier
Snowbound with the Soldier	Jennifer Faye
The Redemption of Rico D'Angelo	Michelle Douglas
The Christmas Baby Surprise	Shirley Jump
Backstage with Her Ex	Louisa George
Blame It on the Champagne	Nina Harrington
Christmas Magic in Heatherdale	Abigail Gordon
The Motherhood Mix-Up	Jennifer Taylor

MEDICAL

Gold Coast Angels: A Doctor's Redemption	Marion Lennox
Gold Coast Angels: Two Tiny Heartbeats	Fiona McArthur
The Secret Between Them	Lucy Clark
Craving Her Rough Diamond Doc	Amalie Berlin

Mills & Boon® Large Print
October 2013

ROMANCE

The Sheikh's Prize	Lynne Graham
Forgiven but not Forgotten?	Abby Green
His Final Bargain	Melanie Milburne
A Throne for the Taking	Kate Walker
Diamond in the Desert	Susan Stephens
A Greek Escape	Elizabeth Power
Princess in the Iron Mask	Victoria Parker
The Man Behind the Pinstripes	Melissa McClone
Falling for the Rebel Falcon	Lucy Gordon
Too Close for Comfort	Heidi Rice
The First Crush Is the Deepest	Nina Harrington

HISTORICAL

Reforming the Viscount	Annie Burrows
A Reputation for Notoriety	Diane Gaston
The Substitute Countess	Lyn Stone
The Sword Dancer	Jeannie Lin
His Lady of Castlemora	Joanna Fulford

MEDICAL

NYC Angels: Unmasking Dr Serious	Laura Iding
NYC Angels: The Wallflower's Secret	Susan Carlisle
Cinderella of Harley Street	Anne Fraser
You, Me and a Family	Sue MacKay
Their Most Forbidden Fling	Melanie Milburne
The Last Doctor She Should Ever Date	Louisa George

0913 GEN STD LP